ALEX

AN EIDOLON BLACK OPS NOVEL: BOOK 1

MADDIE WADE

**Alex: An Eidolon Ghost Ops Novel:
Book 1**

Published by Maddie Wade
Copyright © May 2019 Maddie Wade

Cover: Envy Creative Designs
Editing: Black Opal Editing
Formatting: Black Opal Editing

First edition May © 2019 Maddie Wade

ACKNOWLEDGMENTS

As always there are so many wonderful people who helped bring this book to life. My wonderful beta team, Greta, Lindsey, Rowena, and Deanna and you read my books in such a rough draft and are always so encouraging and supportive. You kick my ass when I need it and don't sugar coat shit. I love you for that. Your feedback is so critical to a good book and I hope I do you proud.

To Anna, Freya, Taryn, Josie, and Aubree you crazy ladies make me smile when I see messenger pop up on my phone. Seriously these chicks are awesome, and you should all go check them out.

My editing and proofing team—Linda and Pam, with a special 'thank you' to Cathy for your thorough read through for plot holes. Thank you for making my rough opal shine.

Thank you to my group Maddie's Minxes, your support especially over the last few months has helped me struggle through a fog of grief and keep going and doing what I love. Special thanks to Rowena, Tracey, Faith, Rachel, Carolyn, Kellie, Maria, Greta,

Deanna, Rihaneh and Linda L for making the group such a friendly place to be.

My ARC Team for not keeping me on edge too long while I wait for feedback.

A big thank you to Itsy Bitsy, and all the bloggers, authors, and friends who promote my books and help others to find my books. Without you I would not be able to do this.

Lastly and most importantly thank you to my readers who have embraced me wholeheartedly and shown a love for the stories in my head. To hear you say that you see my characters as family makes me so humble and proud. I hope you enjoy this new series as much as I do.

To my mum who was the bravest, kindest most loving person I knew. I hope I am half the person you were. I love and miss you more than I can ever say. Not a day goes by when I don't wish you were here, and I could talk to you or hug you. Your loss has rocked my very foundation, but I will carry on and try and make you proud. Until we meet again.

PROLOGUE

THE NIGHT SKY WAS SO CLEAR ALEX THOUGHT HE COULD SEE all the way to the moon. Each tiny sparkling star shone so brightly he thought if he reached out with his fingertips, he could touch them. He watched as Evelyn traced the big dipper in the air and sighed as her body relaxed into his. This right here was the perfect moment.

The night was chilly as Evelyn cuddled deeper into Alex's chest. Her pliant warmth was soft against his hard body. The feeling of rightness and calm he felt whenever she was in his arms ever present. At eighteen, Alex knew precisely what he wanted. His life was planned out and he wanted every dream he had to be shared with his best friend.

Evelyn and Alex had met when he was seven and she was six. Their parents had become friends when Alex's parents fled Cuba and settled in the same neighbourhood in Miami. His seven-year-old-self took one look at Evelyn, the stars aligned, and something had clicked into place. They had been inseparable, getting into scrapes together, having adventures together. Both had other friends too. Alex loved to play ball with the boys, and she would go shopping with her girlfriends, but it always came back to the two of them.

Over time their relationship had evolved from an innocent friendship into something more, something deeper. He loved Evelyn with every bone in his body and he always felt like he could breathe easier when she was with him. At eighteen he knew some thought their love would never last, but he knew his heart. This was more than love. It was two souls always destined to be together. He knew he had loved Evelyn before, and he knew he would love her always.

He was hers and she was his. It was that simple.

"Do you believe in reincarnation?" she asked as he reached for her hand to pull it against him.

He felt her body move as he raised his head and looked down at her. Evelyn tilted her head back to catch his eyes. He loved Evelyn's eyes. They told every emotion, the nuance of colour changing with how she felt. He couldn't see them now in the dark, but he didn't need to see them. He could read her. See the tilt of her lips as he gazed at her.

"*Nena*, what are you talking about?" he asked with affection as he stroked her cheek with his thumb making her shiver. Alex brushed off the delicious feelings her shiver evoked and waited for her to answer him.

"You know. Reincarnation. Do you believe we come back in another body over and over?" she asked as she pushed off his chest and looked down at him as he lounged back on the grass of the river bank where they spent all their free time together. It was their place, their haven from the outside world.

Alex tucked his arm behind his head as he studied her, giving her question real thought before he answered. Evelyn rested her torso against his belly, leaning her chin on his chest as she waited.

"Yes, *nena*. I do. There is no way I can express how much I love you in one lifetime," he answered, and he felt her melt into him as her body became heavier at his words.

"Alex." His name was a whisper, intense with emotion.

He sat up then and pulled her closer until she was sitting between his long legs. She went readily settling against him, his arms cocooning her with his love.

"*Mi nena.*"

She lifted her head at the urgency in his voice. "Yes?" she replied threading her hands around his middle.

He pulled back and she had to reluctantly let go. "You know I love you. You are my world. My life and my best friend. Remember how we talked about me going to college in Europe to work under one of the Michelin Starred Chefs one day?"

"Yes, of course I remember."

He could hear the wariness in her voice and gripped her tighter almost crushing her but never hurting her. "I got a letter this morning. I've been accepted into *Le Cordon Bleu* in Paris," he said excitement tinging his voice.

"Oh my God. You did? Oh, Alex. I'm so happy for you and so proud of you. This is what you always wanted."

"It is," he said slowly and looked away with unease.

"So, what's wrong?" He could hear a caution in her voice he had never heard before.

"How can I go? You don't finish school for another year, and I can't go without you."

"But you must."

Alex let out a breath as he felt her unease leave her. He hated the thought of being apart as much as she did, but it would only be a year and then she could follow him he reasoned.

"Alex, you have to. It's only a year and I'll follow you. You can set up a place for us to live while I apply for art schools in the area."

"I won't be able to afford a lot, but I have some money saved for us," he said into her neck as he held her.

She felt his breath warm on her skin and settled into him. "I don't care if it's one room with a toilet as long as we are together."

"I am going to give you the world," he vowed, and he meant it. He would but all he wanted was her.

"All I want is to be with you until my dying breath." The seriousness of her words belied her age.

"That won't be until we are both very old and grey, *nena*. I have lots I want to do with you and to you before we die," he said with a smile in his voice.

"Yeah? Tell me more."

Alex could hear her delight at his teasing. Evelyn was his soul mate. He didn't need years with her to know that. He didn't care everyone thought they were just kids and it wouldn't last. They knew this was it and nobody would ever understand what they shared.

"Well, I want to cook you your favourite food while you paint a masterpiece. Then I will strip you down and make love to you amidst the paintings and brushes." His lips found her pulse and bit down gently. Her body came alive beneath him as sensation shot through her.

"Sounds a little messy," she said and giggled.

She felt his deep chuckle vibrate up her body making her squirm with desire against him. "Yeah, *mi nena,* scared of a little mess?" he challenged as his lips brushed hers.

"I'm never scared of anything when I'm with you, Alex."

He could see the honesty in her eyes as they lost themselves in a kiss.

CHAPTER ONE

EVER SINCE THE CALL HAD COME IN FROM HER BOSS, EVELYN
had felt an itch on her skin that told her something was very
wrong. Evelyn—also known as Siren to many—was a member of
an elite and secret organisation known only as Zenobi. As such she
was attuned to every single undertone in the air. Right now, her
senses were telling her someone was watching her, and they were
not a friend.

Evelyn resisted the urge to turn around. Years and years of
practice and experience telling her turning and looking would tip
them off. They would know she knew they were watching, and it
would give them the upper hand. Right now, though, they did
because she had no clue what was going on.

Tucking her hands into the pockets of her camel coloured
lambswool coat and hunching into the winter white cashmere
scarf at her neck, Evelyn pushed open the door of the sleek new
building where Zenobi now had their base.

A lot had changed in the last few years with her boss. Roz had
finally got her head out of her ass and married the love of her life
and adopted two adorable girls. It had changed everything for

Zenobi but mainly because the new base had moved from France to England. Mustique was working out of the France office while Roz was based here in the UK.

Evelyn had been flitting between France and England. Her soul was in France but just before Christmas she had found out her heart was England. Her mind went to the tall, handsome man who had stolen her heart as a boy and had never given it back.

Pain lanced through her when she thought of Alex, the ever-familiar knot of grief stealing her breath. Shutting it down with an efficiency born of practice she locked the pain tight knowing it would do her no good to think of him and what they could have had or where their lives could have taken them if only things had been different. But they hadn't and she had learned to live with that years ago. Seeing him in the flesh though had ripped the wound wide open. Now she had to concentrate on healing it closed again before it infected her whole life.

Heated warmth hit her skin making her cheeks tingle as the ice from the cold, northerly wind receded as the door closed behind her. The interior of the new Zenobi office was sleek and classy but with Roz's personal flair in touches here and there. Cream and black leather couches lined the reception area along with a low, glass table. Slashes of red in the artwork on the walls gave it an edgy feel. It suited Zenobi even if nobody knew they were the ones behind the façade. Matching their France office, it had been set up under the name *The Athena Art Gallery* (UK) and was marketed as 'By appointment only' to stop the general public walking in off the street.

Pax, acting as office secretary, smiled as she looked up from where she sat at a large glass reception desk with a MacBook computer in front of her. Pax was tall, slim but curvy, and had a mass of shiny red hair. Today she wore a tight burgundy dress with a vee neckline and cap sleeves. It was classy and sexy and perfectly Pax. She was also deadly. Not in a conventional way although she could shoot and fight as well as the rest of the Zenobi girls, rather, Pax's talent lay more in the finesse with which she knew things or could find them out. Her personal network of contacts in both high and low places was a highly guarded secret and one she didn't share with anybody, even her sisters at Zenobi.

That didn't mean she wouldn't utilise those contacts for her friends though. Pax was a team player, her love for her friends was unquestionable and her loyalty devout.

"Hey, Pax," Evelyn greeted with a smile wondering if Pax knew what was going on.

"Hey, Siren," she responded, her American accent clipped and cultured, her private education shining through despite her trying to hide it. Her lips tilted in a way that said she had a secret nobody knew. It was a familiar look for Pax.

"Is she in?" Evelyn asked not wanting to stop for a chat when the sense of urgency clawing at her was increasing with every second. Pax's face softened slightly and then blanked and Evelyn knew she was right—this wasn't good.

"Yes, go on through. She's expecting you." Pax indicated the door to Roz's office which was closed.

Evelyn didn't waste time. Taking a deep breath, she knocked once, opened the door, and went in.

Roz was sitting crossed legged on the floor surrounded by papers and pictures. Her sleek black cigarette trousers and cream sleeveless blouse were as far as she would go for workwear. If Roz had her way, she would live in either skin-tight jeans or leather biker trousers. She looked up at Evelyn and frowned.

"What's going on, Roz? What's so bad that you couldn't tell me it over the phone?"

Roz stood and hauled herself on to the opposite couch tucking her leg beneath her as she did. Her black stiletto ankle boots looking as sexy as they did lethal. "I got word this morning the British Government, or moreover the British Monarchy, have issued an elimination order on you," she stated with her usual no-nonsense way.

Evelyn masked the shock at her words and spoke with a calmness she wasn't feeling. "Go on," she said knowing there was more.

"They believe you stole something that could cause the downfall of the Monarchy and they want it back and you dead for your part in it."

"I have no idea what they are talking about."

"I know, but for some reason they think you do. Can you think of any reason why your name would come up?"

Roz's faith and belief in her girls was one of the things that made them so loyal to her. That, and Roz had literally saved most of them in some way or another or at the very least given them the skills to survive whatever they were running from. Those who stayed became part of Zenobi and worked deep in the underbelly of the world rescuing people from horrid situations. Sometimes at the behest of governments, sometimes through family members stumbling upon them, and sometimes just because Roz saw fit to do so.

"I helped a woman about six months ago. Her boyfriend was the cousin of a Duke. He was an asshole and was beating her badly, so I helped her get away from him. But he didn't know me or see me."

"Where is she now?"

Evelyn looked up sharply at Roz's tone. "I haven't heard from her in a while. I assumed she was living her life. Do you think he got to her?" Evelyn cursed herself inwardly for not being more diligent about the woman.

"Maybe. I'll get Pax on it. For now, you need to go dark. This is serious business and I won't have your dead body on my conscience. Get yourself somewhere safe and I'll contact you personally through the normal channels with updates. If you need me do the same."

Evelyn's mind raced with her exit strategy. She knew where she would go and how.

She walked to the door but stopped with her hand on the door-knob and twisted back to Roz. "One more thing," Evelyn's voice was soft although the question was vital.

"Yes?"

"Who did they send?"

"Eidolon."

Evelyn nodded slowly as her heart beat faster. Eidolon were the go-to for the government and especially the Monarchy, so it made sense. They also had the best reputation in the business of Black Ops which was what she had just become.

"Okay." She turned to leave.

"Evelyn," Roz called, and she turned back to face Roz. "It was Jack who warned me, but they only have forty-eight hours to deliver and then the contract will go wide. He will set a tail on you though if he hasn't already. If you want to lose them be careful and avoid a certain sexy Cuban hunk."

"Don't worry. I have a feeling I'm the last person he wants to see after New Year's Eve."

Roz inclined her head and studied her. Evelyn felt her chest tighten. "Hmm, well let's get you safe and worry about the rest later."

Leaving the Zenobi offices after collecting her burner phone and a fully equipped go-bag from Pax, Evelyn hustled to her car feeling eyes on her again and knowing in her heart it wasn't Alex or Eidolon.

It DIDN'T TAKE LONG for her to realise she still had her tail. Moving to the car she watched the road as she pulled out. It wouldn't have been obvious to others. Someone with no training would have put it down to coincidence that the same vehicle was behind them still. Evelyn got a quick look at the car and its driver. He wasn't someone she recognised. It didn't take much skill to lose the silver VW Golf tailing her, and before long Evelyn was on a private flight. As she settled back against the warm leather of the seat her mind drifted. Eidolon was hunting her and if they had anything about them, they would send Alex. Alex, the man she'd hardly dared let herself think about. She tilted her head back and recalled their exchange and confrontation on New Year's Eve.

"Alex!"

Fuck! She heard the desperate note in her voice, his name so bittersweet on her lips. Memories of saying his name when they were so much younger. Even after all this time she could hear the sexy sound of his voice in her head as he called her mi nena—my girl. Her hands clinging to him as he watched her with a look of love so intense in his eyes it almost hurt.

"Please, Alex," she said and the scent of him—spice and patchouli with accents of leather and underneath something that was all Alex—wrapped around her like a drug holding her frozen.

She saw his shoulders stiffen, his back going rigid before he turned around. "What can I do for you, Siren?" he asked his voice cold, the tone of it hurting more than she thought it would even though she had been expecting it.

"I just wanted to say how well you look and it's really good to see you." She felt like an inarticulate idiot and immediately wanted to snatch the impersonal words back.

"Really? After fifteen years of me believing you were dead you want to make nice?" She could hear the derision in his voice and couldn't help the wince she gave at his curt words.

"Look, I know you're angry," she began and then paused trying to gather her thoughts, "but I missed you." She reached out to touch his arm as if her hand didn't belong to her. Just one touch and she

was thrown back fifteen years. Her body remembered how he felt and how he made her feel. She ached for him, yearned for him. Every shield she'd ever had tumbled down as she touched the man she had never stopped loving.

"I'm not angry and honestly I hardly thought about you," he said hitting out at her verbally, causing her more pain in one sentence than anyone ever had with a physical blow. Evelyn pulled her hand back as if burned, her pain morphing into anger—an act of protection she had perfected long ago to keep her sanity intact.

"Fine, if that is how you want to play it, fine, but I had my reasons for doing what I did. Looks like both of us changed. You used to be the sweetest, most wonderful man I knew and now you're an arrogant, hurtful prick like all the rest. I'm sorry to have bothered you." She could feel colour rise on her cheeks, the careful check on her temper and her pain a delicate veil right at that moment.

With that she turned and blinked away the moisture she would not allow anyone to see and with her head held high walked away from the love of her life, her soul mate, for the second time. It didn't hurt any less than the first time.

EVELYN CAME awake as the plane began to descend, the memory in her head making her ache. But right now, she had no time for memories or regrets. She was in a fight for her survival and she knew exactly where she had to go and what she had to do. Squaring her shoulders, Evelyn gathered her bag, zipped up her quilted jacket and exited the plane.

CHAPTER TWO

THE COLD BIT AT HIS CHEEKS AS SLEET AND RAIN PELTED HIS skin and Alex welcomed it. The weather matched his mood. Valentine's Day was coming up and as per usual his thoughts were on Evelyn. The difference was they weren't on the Evelyn of his memories. No. His thoughts were on the sexy woman who had walked away from him on New Year's Eve and hadn't looked back.

He was still pissed he hadn't known she was Zenobi. But it made a kind of poetic sense that the elusive Siren he'd heard about at previous meetings and associations with the female assassin group would be the woman he had loved. It was the final kick in the balls from her.

He hunched into his coat as he checked his watch when it beeped. A call from Jack at this time of night meant only one thing —a mission had come in and he thanked God for it. He needed the distraction despite the fact he had only just left a shit-storm in Syria. His body may be tired but his mind needed to keep busy so he wouldn't give in to the anger and feelings pummelling him.

He diverted from his early morning walk that had become a regular thing now his insomnia had hit an all-time high. A few hours a night was all his body granted him before dreams of a woman screaming and haunted eyes merged and all he saw were visions of Evelyn, bruised and looking like a broken doll, swimming in front of him.

He had no clue what the dreams meant. He had never seen her in such a way but every time he woke, Alex couldn't shake the feelings of grief and anger that he hadn't saved her. Punching in the code at the front gate of Eidolon, Alex put his eye up to the scanner and walked through as the gate slid back allowing him entry.

At four-thirty in the morning the place was dark from the outside, but he knew Jack was in his office. The man practically lived there—not that he was judging, his life was just as sad these days. Not bothering to stop for coffee knowing Jack would have some ready, he made his way straight for his boss's office and knocked on the door.

"Come in."

Alex opened the door and Jack looked up at him from his seat at the desk.

"That was quick," Jack commented as Alex walked to the side table along the wall where Jack always kept the coffee pot.

"Yeah. I was out for a walk."

"At four-thirty in the morning?"

"Yeah. I couldn't sleep. You know how it is." He hoped Jack got the hint that he didn't want to talk about it.

"Hmm." After making the noncommittal sound, Jack pulled a file from his desk that had the Palace seal on the front. "I have a job for you. It's highly sensitive and will involve a lot of finesse from a diplomatic standpoint. I also believe there has been a mistake and that's why I'm trusting you with this."

"What is the job?" Alex wasn't fazed by Jack's words. It wouldn't be the first time Eidolon had handled such a mission.

"Before I tell you I need to know you have your head on

straight. This is the first time I'm going to try and save the intended target rather than simply taking them out," Jack said holding the file close.

Now Alex was intrigued. He sat back and rested his ankle on his knee as he watched Jack for a clue but got nothing. The man was the absolute master at hiding his feelings. With dark hair and blue eyes Jack was the poster boy for tall dark and brooding. His clipped British accent was cultured and self-assured giving him the impression of superiority which he wore like a general. "My head is on fine and I resent the implication," he replied coldly not liking what Jack was suggesting.

"Keep your hair on. I have my reasons." Jack pushed the file towards Alex but kept his hand on it. "This is the target. Your job is to protect and disprove the allegations made against them," he said with a frown.

"Why would we do that?"

"Because I owe them a debt and this is me repaying that debt." Jack let go of the file so Alex could open it.

Lifting the file Alex had the strangest sensation that opening it would alter the course of his life forever. Flipping it open he barely held back a gasp as he saw the face of the woman who had haunted his dreams for the last fifteen years—Evelyn Garcia was his target.

He looked up swiftly and caught the look of caution in Jack's eyes. Jack had a way of reading people. It made him a good boss, a good friend, and the best damn operative Alex had ever worked with. All the Eidolon men were. Even Will—the owner of the company and Jack's brother—had proven himself an asset in the field. Technically a computer geek and hacker second to none Will had made millions with his inventions. Keeping Jack in the dark he had secretly started Eidolon, then recruited Jack to lead and run it.

Now Jack was a partner, but things hadn't changed at all. Will still worked for Fortis Security as their tech expert. A respected company owned by ex-SAS man Zack Cunningham, who was an old colleague of Jack's from his SAS days. Eidolon did a lot of work with them and the teams got on well, even went drinking together on occasion. Although generally the Fortis jobs weren't as dark as what Eidolon handled.

Eidolon had contracts with the Monarchy and the British Government that were buried so deep nobody would ever find a link. Jack even had the Palace on speed dial. No, the jobs Eidolon did were so black they blended into oblivion and the only other company like that was Zenobi, an all-female elite group of assassins for hire.

Zenobi was a major pain in their ass and had been for years. The competitiveness between them bordered on hostile although there had been a thaw of late facilitated in part by their links to Fortis Security. Being forced to work together had made both teams cease hostilities for now.

Alex glanced back at the file in his hands not for the first time wondering how he had never known Evelyn was Zenobi. *How did I not know she was alive for fifteen fucking torturous years and working as a motherfucking assassin?*

Years spent missing her, mourning her, aching for her. It made him furious to think how she must have known he was alive, and she'd never got in touch, not even to say she was okay. He felt himself grip the file so hard the ends curled as he fought to control his temper again. Exhaustion battered him. As he closed his eyes the vision of her instantly assailed him. Despite his fury and his anger, he still fucking wanted her. Still felt the need to run his fingers across her soft skin, curl his hand around her hair, hear her cry his name as she came on his cock.

That was lust. He could accept that to a degree. It was the ache he felt when he saw her walk away and had known he had hurt her that was the problem. How he wanted to drag her back into his arms after their exchange on New Year's Eve and tell her he was sorry and would never hurt her again if only she would stay this time. But his pride would not allow that no matter what his heart wanted.

HE STOOD WATCHING *the woman he had loved since she was six years old as she laughed and chatted with Zack and Ava. She had changed so much and yet hardly at all. She was still the most beautiful woman he had ever met, still had that dimple in her left cheek when she smiled, still quirked her head the way he loved when she was listening to someone, and yet she was not the same.*

The woman he had loved had been soft and gentle and wouldn't hurt a fly much less kill a man in cold blood and then walk away. Evelyn had disappeared a little under fifteen years ago, taken from their village on the same night he had proposed and had never been seen again.

He had spent years searching for her with no luck and then suddenly, she popped into his life from nowhere throwing him into chaos. It made him inexplicably angry that she seemed so unaffected. As if what they'd had was insignificant, worthless, when he'd spent his adulthood pining for her, missing her goofy laugh and the way she made him feel.

But Siren as she was now, acted as if he was nobody and nothing to her, and yet he still felt his body stir every time he caught sight of her. Alex took a swig of his gin and tonic and then slammed the glass down, almost smashing it as she flirted with Gunner. He needed another fucking drink. He stalked to the bar and felt eyes on him as he passed by them, deliberately ignoring them all.

"Alex!"

Fuck, her voice, the way she said his name made his body ache to touch her, to make her remember how it had been between them when they were barely seventeen. Even after all this time, he could hear the sweet sound of her voice as she came, her hands clinging to him, a look of love so intense in her eyes that it almost blinded him.

"Please, Alex," she said and the scent she had always worn, vanilla and jasmine wrapped around his senses like a drug holding him immobile.

Stiffening his stance, he turned around. "What can I do for you, Siren?" he asked, is voice cold.

"I just wanted to say how well you look and it's really good to see you," she said looking injured at his curt tone.

"Really? After fifteen years of me believing you were dead, you want to make nice?" he spat with derision and saw her flinch.

"Look, I know you're angry, but I missed you," she said reaching out to touch his arm.

The touch sent a thousand tiny electrical pulses through his arm as memories flooded him. Hurt and anger doused them in cold water as he shook off her hand. "I'm not angry, and honestly, I hardly thought about you," he said hitting out and knowing he had scored a direct hit when she stiffened.

"Fine, if that is how you want to play it, fine, but I had my reasons for doing what I did. Looks like both of us changed. You used to be the sweetest, most wonderful man I knew and now you're an arrogant, hurtful prick like all the rest. I'm sorry to have bothered you," she said as colour rose on her cheeks.

He watched trying to decide what to do, annoyed with how turned on he was by her fury as she walked away. Like a fool, he let her go.

ALEX PULLED himself back from his reverie and realised he had not spoken since Jack handed him the file. He couldn't allow himself to slip now, not when her life was at stake. He had watched, stunned, as she had saved Jack from a shot that would have killed him taking the man down with a calm, clean shot to the head that *his* Evelyn would never have taken. His first glimpse of the woman she had become had nearly brought him low but overshadowing that had been abject relief that she was alive.

Then she had looked at him and he knew—*he knew*—from the lack of surprise and shock on her face that she had known where he was and had let him suffer. Then came the anger which even now, he couldn't mask.

But now he had an opportunity, a chance to get the answers from her that he needed. Mainly why the fuck did she leave him fifteen years ago with no word, where did she go, and what had made her become Siren?

"I'll do it," he said rising from his seat.

Jack leaned back in his chair and watched him with a cool look. "You have forty-eight hours and then they'll send in a second team I can't control. I owe her for saving my life and this is me repaying the favour. It will also balance the books between us and Zenobi. Get Siren safe and find out what the fuck is going on. I've reached out to Roz to warn her so she may have gone dark. Her last known location was an airstrip near the French Alps called Courchevel."

"France." He grinned feeling a lightness that he hadn't felt in a long time. Maybe she hadn't forgotten them after all. "Okay. I have a starting point. I'm going to contact Will and ask him to run a trace. I assume Roz doesn't know where she went after the airstrip?"

"If she does, she isn't saying."

"No problem. I'll find her. Normal procedure?" Alex asked referring to the procedure they ran for dark Black Ops.

"Yes, don't go dark until you have her though in case anyone is watching. For now, it's business as normal. Be seen but when you find her, you'll need to move quickly. I will have the plane readied and file a flight plan. Your flight departs in two hours."

"No problem. Let me speak to geek boy and then I'm going to hit the gym for a bit. Do I have cover?"

"Blake, Reid, and Liam will shadow you but don't acknowledge them until I say so. I'll oversee things from here."

Alex stood and moved away but then stopped. "I won't mess this up."

"I never doubted you would, or you wouldn't be on this job."

Alex nodded and took out his phone and hit dial. "Geek boy, wake up. I have a favour to ask," he said into the phone when it was answered by a sleepy Will Granger.

CHAPTER THREE

WILL OPENED THE DOOR LOOKING HALF ASLEEP AND SLIGHTLY pissed off, his black hair which was too long in Alex's opinion falling over his face.

"Thanks for doing this, Will." Alex stepped past him into the warmth of the hallway which by the looks of it had been decorated since he was there last. Will had met the love of his life last year and was now firmly ensconced in domestic bliss.

"No problem," he grumbled over a yawn making Alex chuckle.

He followed as Will led him into the kitchen where he could smell coffee brewing. It was then Alex realised he hadn't touched the coffee he had poured in Jack's office. He'd been keen to get started and find Evelyn. He smiled when he saw Will's police detective girlfriend Aubrey who was already dressed for work.

"Morning, Alex." She smiled as Will walked over to her scratching his belly like a sleepy cat and then slid his arms around her waist as he stood behind her and leaned his chin on her shoulder. It was an intimate gesture and one which made Alex's chest tighten.

"Morning, Aubrey. Sorry to spring by so early," he said suddenly wanting away from the domestic scene in front of him.

"It's okay. I have to be at work at six am anyway. This way Will can get a head start on stripping the wallpaper in the spare room." She grinned at Will who frowned and sighed but Alex could see he would do anything for Aubrey. *Well, he did fucking steal a plane and fly halfway around the world to rescue her from drug lords.*

"I keep telling her we could hire someone to do all this, but she just likes to see me suffer."

"But then it wouldn't be personal, and I want this to be ours," she replied as she handed Alex a mug of hot steaming coffee.

Will rolled his eyes then kissed her softly before disentangling himself from her and walking towards the hallway that led to his home office. "Come on, Alex. Let's see what you need before she has me sanding floors," he said ducking as a tea towel came flying at his head.

"Missed," he called, and Alex heard her laugh softly.

Aubrey and Will were a great couple but on paper a complete mismatch. She was a copper, Will was a tatted up ex-con turned tech mogul, with millions in the bank. Their differences couldn't be compared to Wills and Jack's though. The two brothers couldn't be more different if they tried but after years of estrangement, they were closer than ever now.

Alex was glad to see it. Family was everything in his book even if you didn't see them as often as you wanted. He followed Will into his office which was a home office like no other. It looked more like mission control at NASA. The room housed four colossal computer monitors, two large servers in the corner with fans whirring to keep them cold, and a whole host of other things that Alex had no care to understand. What Will did was over and above what the average person could grasp.

Will sat down in a black leather executive chair and pulled

himself up to the desk hitting keys on the keyboard as he did. "What is it you need, Alex?" he asked twisting to look at him with an open expression.

"I need you to look into anything under the name Evelyn Garcia or Evelyn Fernandez. That was her mum's maiden name," he said.

"Okay. Any more details? Age? Date of birth, etcetera?" Will's fingers started to fly over the keys.

"She might have property in France, USA, or the UK or possibly Cuba as it's our place of birth, but it is less likely. Her date of birth is the same as mine. Tenth of June, but she's a year younger." His mind flew to the last birthday they had spent together.

"ALEX, WHERE ARE WE GOING?" Evelyn asked with a giggle as she held tight to his hand, the blindfold he had placed over her eyes making it impossible for her to see.

"Just wait and see." He chuckled as he led her down the path towards the surprise he had planned. It was her eighteenth birthday and he wanted it to be special. He was leaving for France in two months and had no idea how he was going to cope without seeing her every day. She had been his life for twelve perfect years and now they would be apart for twelve months with only short visits in between. He pushed the thought away as he moved to the blanket he had laid out for them helping her sit, before removing the blindfold. Evelyn blinked her eyes, the light from the hundreds of tealight candles he had lit showing the joy on her face.

"Oh, Alex, it's perfect," she said throwing her arms around him and kissing him hard.

He caught her and held her tight as he took control of the kiss feeling her body soften into his, her fingers threading through his hair. He pulled back not wanting to get to carried away before he had given her the birthday gift he had planned.

"Ready for your present?" he asked excitement bubbling inside him.

"Yes," she said clapping her hands.

His Evelyn loved presents and surprises. He smiled and hoped this would be one she would never forget. Leaning back, he reached for the box and held it out for her. He watched with his heart in his mouth as she opened the box to reveal his grandmother's engagement ring. She had given it to him two years before, making him promise to only give it to the woman he had given his heart to freely. She had died three months later, and he had held on to the ring knowing one day it would belong to Evelyn.

Her eyes came to him in question as he took her hand in his.

"Evelyn, I know we're young, but I've loved you since the day we met. You're my best friend, my soul mate, the only person I want by my side for eternity. Marry me?" he asked and saw her face crease into a smile as tears ran down her cheeks.

"Of course, I'll marry you," she said once again throwing herself into his arms.

She pulled away and he fitted the ring onto her finger, the antique white gold ring with three diamonds along the top and tiny diamonds along the shoulders fit her perfectly. He had the wedding band to go with it and couldn't wait until they were both on her finger for good.

"Oh, it's so beautiful," she said with tears in her eyes.

"Not as beautiful as you, mi nena," said as he admired her knowing in his heart that he would carry this precious memory to the grave as being the best birthday of his life.

"What will my parents say though?" she said biting her lip.

Evelyn's parents were strict and although they loved Alex, they believed she was too young to decide her future.

"Well, that's where present two comes in." He handed her a second slightly larger box.

She looked up at him and grinned before opening it. Inside was a circular pendant in white gold. The middle was hollow like a wedding ring and had tiny crystals around the outside. "Alex, this is perfect."

"Turn it over," he said nerves fluttering in his chest as she read the words on the back.

Mi nena was etched along the top curve with Evelyn Martinez along the bottom. It was an assumption he knew, but he hoped she would like it. "It opens up, look!" Evelyn opened the circular pendant and found a plain white gold wedding band inside. It meant she could wear it, and nobody would know the significance except them.

"This is..." She couldn't continue as her tears blocked her throat almost making him cry with her. Instead he hauled her into his arms and held her close. They ate under the stars surrounded by flowers and candlelight. Alex fed her fresh cut fruit after they had dined on Cuban sandwiches and sweet flan.

"Nena Garcia or Nena Martinez try those too," he said to Will his trip down memory lane leaving him shaken.

"Okay. So, I take it we're cyberstalking?" he asked, and Alex nodded. "What's the story with you two anyway?" Will's directness always surprised Alex.

"That story is one to be told over something much stronger than coffee and we don't have time. Just call me as soon as you have anything. We have forty-eight hours to find her or the shit will hit the fan. You need to talk to Jack about this one as it involves Zenobi and with you working for Fortis it might complicate things with Kanan."

Kanan was Roz's husband and also an ex-SIS agent. He was

also very protective of his wife and with Will being part owner of the company charged with taking out one of her girls it could get awkward.

"Hey, anything to get out of stripping wallpaper, even my brother's ugly face on a Saturday morning." Will grinned before sobering. "I'll work on this non-stop. Whatever is going on with you and Siren it isn't finished, not by a long shot."

Alex nodded. A truer word was never spoken he thought as he left Will to work and headed for the gym at Eidolon. He needed a workout preferably one where punches were thrown, and he knew just the men to help him.

CHANGING into shorts and a loose vest Alex made his way to the fully equipped gym. Liam was in the ring with Mitch, their firearms and weapons expert. He had worked for SO19 the UK Police Firearms Unit at the London Met for ten years before joining Eidolon. At six-foot three and 200 pounds of pure muscle Mitch was a beast in a fight.

Born in Peckham South-East London he had spent the first part of his youth in a gang on his council estate before finally getting his act together when he was twenty. Now at forty-five he was the oldest member of the team and took great pleasure in whooping everyone's asses just to prove he was still a badass. The team frequently got their own back by putting up pictures of Idris Elba who he had been mistaken for more than once.

Waggs, currently holding his own in the ring against Liam, was an ex-Green Beret and the team medic. Tall, though not as tall as Mitch, with short blonde hair and piercing blue eyes, Waggs was the quiet one of the group, and more serious than the others. He was a sound guy and had patched all of them up at some point or other.

Blake and Reid were using the weights and Reid lifted his head in greeting when he walked in.

"Alex." Blake greeted him with a smile. He was the baby at thirty and seemed to always have women literally eating out of his hands.

"They been in long?"

"A few rounds, I think. Liam has this one. He has a bug up his ass and it's making him bitchy," Blake remarked of the cockney that was usually the life and soul of the group.

"Fancy a few rounds?" Alex asked them both knowing one would surely take him up on his offer.

"Sure. You hankering for an ass-kicking?" Reid headed for the second ring and tossed his shirt on the floor revealing his heavily tattooed torso.

"Dream on, Captain Kirk," Alex replied and watched Reid scowl at the nickname they had given him. Kirk as a first name was just begging for a Star Trek joke.

Thirty minutes later both he and Reid were sweating as they traded hit after hit, kick after kick, neither one managing to get the upper hand.

Mitch, Waggs, and Liam were watching the fight taking bets as Blake called time. He and Reid shook hands as Jack walked into the gym. He looked at Alex and beckoned him over with a nod of his head. Wiping his face with a towel, Alex jogged over, his instincts telling him this was it. They had a lead on Evelyn. He felt wired and full of energy despite the workout he had just had.

"Yeah?"

"We found her and by *we*, I mean my geek brother found her. She has a chalet in Courchevel under the name Nena Fernandez."

Everything inside Alex settled for just a second before he remembered the clock was ticking. "Let's go." He headed for the shower. It was time to find Evelyn and figure out what the fuck was going on.

CHAPTER FOUR

SECURING THE SUPPLIES SHE HAD BOUGHT IN HER BACKPACK, Evelyn slid her boots into the skis and set off towards her home. The two-bedroom wooden chalet that she owned deep in the mountains of Courchevel was more than a bolt hole—it was her sanctuary. A place nobody knew about. At least, nobody that was alive. Not even Roz knew of this place, which was how she wanted it.

Manoeuvring over the fresh snow that glistened so brightly it was almost blinding, Evelyn used every ounce of skill she had to negotiate the steep slope on this side of the mountain. This area was classed as a black diamond run and therefore most skiers avoided it. Only the most experienced or thrill-seeking skiers came here, and her chalet was deeper in the mountain where even they dared not go.

Snow was beginning to fall steadily as she crossed the boundary that led to her property. Her eye moved to the tripwire that ran across the tree line and she was satisfied that nobody had gotten through her security. Pulling to a stop at the front of her chalet, Evelyn eyed the pile of wood and noted she needed to stock up. With the cold front that was predicted and the new dumping of snow they were going to get later that night, she needed to make sure she had enough wood to keep her going for however long she would be there.

Having checked in with Roz while she was in Courchevel getting food and water she knew that they had no update on who or why the British Government had issued a kill order on her. Unclipping her skis, she stamped her feet to get the excess snow from her boots and clothing before opening the door and stopping dead in her tracks.

Every hair on her body stood on end as she felt the air in her small home vibrate with electricity. Someone was inside. She had missed the signs, or worse there were none, which meant whoever was inside was a professional. With silent movements, Evelyn slid her hand into her jacket and withdrew her firearm. The weight of it felt good in her hand. Her breathing evened out and she listened for any sound that would tell her where they were and maybe how many.

Inwardly she cursed her bulky jacket that restricted her movements. The nylon of the ski suit sounded like crackling tinfoil in the silence of the room. She was at a considerable disadvantage, but it wouldn't be the first time and hopefully wouldn't be the last. Slinking forward, her back to the wall, she checked behind the island in the open plan kitchen before moving along the hallway that led to the bedrooms and bathroom. Checking the spare room and then the bathroom, which was clear, Evelyn realised whoever was there was in her bedroom.

The thought made her strangely angry. How dare they invade her private space and more importantly it was where the emergency exit for the house was hidden. Her secret escape route for when this sort of thing happened. With her back to the wall she took a breath and in one lightning quick movement spun, kicked her beautiful wooden bedroom door in, and trained her weapon on thin air.

Then out of nowhere a weight hit her from behind tackling her to the ground. Not ready to die yet Evelyn threw back with her head as she lost her grip on her gun sending it flying beneath the bed. She heard the thud as her head encountered a hard chest confirming that it was a man behind her. A whoosh of air rushed out his lungs from the impact. He grabbed her arms and manacled her wrists as she tried to twist and free herself from his firm grip. Evelyn caught sight of a black-clad arm and knew she had to use surprise not strength or she would lose.

Going perfectly still for a second, she waited and then pushed up with her hips to throw the man off her. A yelp of pain had her smiling as she realised she had caught him right where it hurt before another realisation hit her.

"For fuck's sake, Evelyn, pack it in with that shit." It was the voice of the man who had stalked her dreams since she'd been old enough to feel desire.

"Alex?" she asked thinking her mind was playing tricks on her.

"Yes. Alex." He eased himself off her not letting go of her wrists until he was out of the strike zone. Instantly she was on her feet. Rounding on him she saw he had moved further away and had a cautious look in his eye.

"Why are you here? And how the hell did you find me?" Her brisk questions were a way of masking the fact that she was having a profound reaction to being so close to him again. When they had met before Christmas, she had been expecting it, had armoured herself and donned the persona of Siren, but this unexpected visit left her reeling.

"I've come for you, Evelyn."

His reply was cold, and her eyes shot to his at the hostility she heard in his voice. Was he here to kill her? Was he going against Jack's orders or were they Jack's orders and he'd lied to Roz? *No, Jack wouldn't do that.* She had saved his life and he wouldn't repay that by killing her. He wasn't that sort of man—she didn't think.

"Why?" she asked trying to buy time while she got her bearings.

This Alex was not one she knew. This Alex was cold, calm, and lethal. He had done and seen things her Alex never would have, and it hurt her heart to think about that and how he had changed as a result of what she'd done. Regret was a lancing pain through her chest.

Through it all she could still see glimpses of the boy she had loved with all her heart. His features had matured and hardened, his strong jaw defined and proud, but his eyes had lines along the edges showing he laughed often. Full lips that had brought her so much pleasure looked soft enough to kiss. His hands were calloused now, the feel of them on her wrists leaving a tingling sensation behind. She knew that was due to the effect he had on her, not that he had hurt her in any way.

He regarded her silently, his head tilted in a way that it always had when he was thinking. It took her back to a time when she knew his every little quirk and he hers. His body language seemed relaxed now as he watched her, his hands hanging loosely at his sides, but she was no fool and she knew every muscle in his body was poised and ready to move.

"That's a good question and not one that has a simple answer, Siren."

He'd spat the name out and she flinched hating the fact he used it. She never wanted to be Siren to Alex. His tone was angry and again, she wondered if he would hurt her. Her gut told her no, but she didn't trust her instincts with Alex, everything was skewed by their history. She glanced towards the bed and the gun that was poking out from under it.

He followed her glance with his eyes, and she knew her time was up. Diving towards the bed she grabbed for the gun, but he got there first wrestling it out of reach before catching her body in the steel of his arms, pinning them to her sides. His body was hard and yet so familiar to her as his scent hit her. Not aftershave, just Alex. Pain caused her throat to clog at the familiar warmth she felt in those seconds before she fought against his hold trying desperately to get away before she burst into stupid tears and begged him to forgive her.

His mouth moved closer to her ear, the tickle of his breath making her shiver as he held her immobile against him. Defiant she looked up and saw the raging storm in his warm hazel eyes turn them a pale green as his jaw ticked with barely contained fury. His words when they came were soft, like a caress over her heated skin. She felt it through the cumbersome jacket which she was now glad she had on as a barrier to the sexy man imprisoning her.

"It seems we are not as attuned as we once were. I was looking at the bed thinking how much I wanted to lay you down and fuck you on it, but it seems you were looking at the gun underneath and wondering how to kill me with it." He pushed away from her in disgust.

Evelyn sucked in a breath fighting the effect his crass words had on her, but it was useless. The image of him fucking her on her bed was raw and vivid in her head. A buzz of desire settled in her belly at the erotic images he had evoked.

"I have no desire to kill you, Alex. I was protecting myself that's all." She was proud of the way her voice held as she faced him, her head held high.

"Protect you from who? Me?" His voice was so cold she almost shivered. "You honestly think I would hurt you?"

Evelyn saw the look of hurt as it slid across his features and regret filled her. Had she thought that? No, maybe not but she couldn't think straight with him here and especially not after the images he had conjured in her mind. So instead of answering she walked from the room heading for the kitchen. Once there, she flicked the coffee machine on as she began to shed her ski suit. She felt him behind her but didn't turn. Once her suit was off, she hung it by the door and returned to the island putting it between her and Alex.

"Coffee?" she asked, and he nodded stiffly. Evelyn began to busy herself making coffee trying not to look at Alex. "So why are you here?"

As she handed over the mug his fingers brushed hers and she felt it in her toes. How did he make such a simple light touch feel like a sexual caress? Evelyn grinned as he took a sip and grimaced.

"Glad to see not everything has changed. You still make the worst coffee known to man," he said with a wince.

"Still a coffee snob I see," she countered, and his warm chuckle filled her heart with warmth. She smiled at him and he returned it, the years falling away as if they had never been apart.

Then she sobered knowing it would be so easy to fall in love with this new Alex. It would be as easy as it had been to fall for the old one. Feelings were rushing at her, a myriad of memories flashing in her mind.

"We aren't those innocent kids anymore. Too much has changed." She didn't realise she'd said it out loud until Alex spoke.

"No, we aren't but not everything has changed." He rounded the island placing his mug on the counter.

Her heart sped up as he moved closer, but she held her ground not wanting him to see how he affected her. "Everything that matters has changed."

He moved closer, his body crowding her against the kitchen island but not touching her. "Not everything."

Evelyn felt her breath catch in her throat as his head dipped and she couldn't move, not even if her life depended on it. Her heart was pounding so hard in her chest that she thought she might faint.

His lips were nearly on hers when he spoke again. "You are still the most beautiful woman I have ever met," he whispered as his lips brushed hers in a light caress before every light in the cabin went out.

CHAPTER FIVE

ALEX TENSED FOR A SPLIT SECOND BEFORE GRABBING EVELYN and yanking her behind the kitchen island as the ping of a bullet hitting the marble resounded in the silent room.

"Fuck. They didn't waste any time." Alex's brain raced for exit routes. He had two firearms and three K-bar knives on him. He knew that whoever was out there was experienced and highly trained.

The silence that followed the bullet was worse than being fired on.

"We need to move—now!" he said urgently grabbing her hand and palming his gun.

"I have an escape hatch in the bedroom."

Evelyn pulled her hand from his and grabbed a gun that had been taped to the underside of the island. Alex buried the shock he felt at her words. Evelyn was prepared for this which begged the question of why and what had happened to her to make her this way. He had no time to try and gather his thoughts though because she took off running, leaving him no choice but to follow her.

Crouching low to the ground they made it to the hallway as a hail of bullets rained down on them from an automatic weapon. Wood splintered and fell on them as he dropped down beside Evelyn between the bed and the wardrobe.

Evelyn turned and opened the wardrobe, hitting a button below the hinge. A drawer popped open that was filled with weapons and ammo. She thrust two handguns and a small semi-automatic gun at him, and Alex wasted no time with the thousands of questions that were going through his mind and locked the clip into the weapon as Evelyn did the same.

"Which way? We need to get out of here," he said looking at her and seeing a woman he didn't recognise.

"Here."

Alex stayed close as she crawled on her belly to the bed, pushed the coverlet aside, opened a latch, and pulled back a small trap door big enough for one person at a time to go through. It was a vertical drop and he couldn't see the bottom through the fading light.

"This leads us out about a mile further down the mountain," she said as she began to climb down.

Alex said nothing as he watched the door his firearm aimed. "Go. I'm right behind you." He felt her move as he listened to the sound of boots kicking the front door down. It was holding better than he had expected but then again it was probably reinforced titanium knowing this new Evelyn. The sound of her feet as they hit solid ground had him moving. Climbing to the edge, he gripped the door and pulled it closed as he let himself drop to ground inside the tunnel.

Evelyn snapped a glow stick usually used for camping and the dark tunnel was illuminated in green light. It was crude but it worked. Reaching out she grabbed his hand, but he didn't have time to enjoy the moment as she pulled him deeper into the escape route. Their feet thudded on the cold earth, the smell of soil and earth sharp in his nose. When they had been moving for a few minutes he realised he could no longer hear the sounds of gunfire.

Deeming it safe to speak he asked the obvious question. "What is this place?" He couldn't see Evelyn's face as there wasn't space for them to walk side by side, but he felt her tense and she let go of his hand. It made him inexplicably angry that she was shutting him out. He was about to call her on it when the tunnel came to a sudden end and the light from outside filtered in through the concealed entrance. Evelyn moved to climb out first, but he stopped her with a hand on her elbow.

"Let me go first."

Alex gave her no time to argue before he pushed her aside and stopped to listen for any signs of an ambush. Hearing nothing, he slowly pushed aside the heavy wooden logs that were stacked up and covered in snow and eased his way out. Satisfied that nobody was waiting to blow his head off he climbed out and turned to offer Evelyn his hand, but she was already out and brushing the snow from her knees. It was then he noticed that she was only wearing a base layer.

Taking off his jacket he tried to hand it to her. "Here."

She looked up about to speak when a powerful explosion rocked the mountain behind them. Looking up he saw smoke billowing from where her little chalet had been and swore inwardly. Fuckers didn't need to do that, but it meant that in their haste to destroy the place they hadn't found the escape route. Glancing back at Evelyn he saw grief and pain sharp on her pretty features before she masked it.

"I'm sorry about your place," he said as he handed her the jacket which she now took with a silent nod.

"It's just wood and stone," she replied bravely as she shrugged on the jacket, tiny lines around her pinched mouth showing him how much she was hurting.

Bitterness weighed him down at the ease with which she lied

to him. "Don't do that, Evelyn. We may have been apart for fifteen years, but I know you." He pulled her into his chest and brought both sides of the jacket she had slipped on together and zipped it up to her chin so that the cold wouldn't touch her before he carried on. "You loved that place and it meant something to you. Don't hide that from me."

Alex let go even though what he wanted to do was finish what he had started in her cabin and moved off towards the direction of the village below. The air was quiet, and he thanked God that the explosion hadn't caused an avalanche. It was a short hike, but the temperature was dropping fast, and they needed to find a place to stay. He started walking and Evelyn fell in step beside him.

They walked for fifteen minutes before she spoke. "You're right. It did mean something to me. It belonged to a friend of mine and when he died, he left it to me. The escape route was his idea to keep me safe."

Alex locked every muscle in his body in an attempt not to react to her words. He had so many questions to that but if he asked them all at once he knew she would shut down.

So instead he just made the obvious statement even though it hurt more than it should. "You loved him." He angled his head towards her waiting for her to deny it, but she didn't.

"Very much," she replied and the knife of pain in his solar plexus was agony.

The rest of the trudge through the snow was made in silence but it wasn't awkward, rather contemplative. Alex tried to keep his thoughts on the mission ahead of him. Keeping Evelyn safe was already proving to be a bigger task than he had expected. He couldn't afford to let his mind wander to the mystery man that Evelyn had loved that wasn't him. She still wanted him though and maybe that was all they had now, but his desperate desire to take the sadness from her eyes and to make her smile were not the actions of a man who wanted to get laid. They were the actions of a man who cared.

As they neared civilisation Alex pondered his next move. He had obviously picked up a tail at some point and been followed to the cabin. Nobody but Jack, and Will knew about the cabin, except the Eidolon team that was shadowing him and now Evelyn. That meant he had slipped up and that was not going to happen again. The resort of Courchevel was made up of five main villages that were connected by ski lifts and shuttle buses. Each had its own unique character. Courchevel 1850 was for the rich and famous. Exclusive shops and high-end restaurants, a few of which Alex would love to explore if he had ever had time. He was staying in Courchevel Moriond which was lower down the slope and maintained a busy nightlife and a high tourist population making it the perfect place to disappear. They now found themselves in Courchevel Le Praz where most of the ski instructors had homes. He couldn't risk going back to his hotel, but they needed some-where to stay for the night before he got hold of Jack to arrange an extraction, including a new passport for Evelyn.

He looked around hating being exposed. "We need to find somewhere to stay." They had dumped most of their weapons before they hit the village only carrying their knives and one handgun each.

"I know a place," she said and started walking towards a café that was brimming with warm light and laughter.

Alex had no choice but to follow her. She moved with confi-dence and grace he didn't remember from their younger years. Evelyn had always been petite and still was but now she moved like a sleek cat. Even in the thick ski jacket she was attracting the attention of men around her.

Her codename of Siren suited her because without a word she called to a man. The sway of her hips, the flick of her hair, and she had him under her spell and only some of it was contrived, the rest was due to the woman she had become.

Slipping into the back of the café, Evelyn moved through the kitchen as if she was expected with barely a person stopping except to smile at her. Going through a door at the back he found they were in a small hallway with stairs leading up to a locked painted blue door.

"What is this?"

Evelyn took a key from under the ledge on a storage heater. "A friend owns it. They're out of town and won't mind us staying here."

Alex stiffened again as jealousy swam through his blood like a shark seeking prey. "Are you sure he won't mind your ex staying here?" His tone was brittle and snappy.

Evelyn turned her head to look at him as she put her foot on the bottom step her eyebrow quirked in question her lip twitching. "Are you jealous, Alex?" Incredulous amusement moved over her face.

"No," he denied vehemently even though he recognised that was exactly what he was.

"*Oh my God.* You *are* jealous. You can lie to yourself but not to me, Alex Martinez." She laughed as she slid the key in the lock and opened the door.

"I am not lying." Alex slipped an arm around her waist and pulled her around so he could see her pretty face. Her smile threatened his composure, and at that moment, he didn't care who this place belonged to—he was just happy to have made her smile.

Her laughter filled the apartment and Alex knew he would move heaven and earth to keep that in his life.

CHAPTER SIX

THE LAST THIRTY-SIX HOURS HAD BEEN A ROLLERCOASTER OF emotions for Evelyn. Pain, grief, happiness, desire, and anger to name a few. She had run the gamut and it left her feeling exhausted.

After arriving at her friend Mariam's flat above Café Belle Vie, she and Alex had put in calls to their teams. Her to Roz to let her know what had happened. Roz had lost her cool on the phone as Evelyn knew she would. Roz was a tough operator, probably the most lethal female assassin ever known, but those that knew her well also knew she had a soft side. If she loved you or classed you as one of her own then she would die before allowing anyone to threaten you. Every single person who worked for Zenobi became like family, especially to Roz. She was the patriarch, and despite her horrific past she had a huge capacity for love and treated her girls with the protective nature of a mother hen—albeit a mother hen who could kill a man with a hair tie and not flinch.

Most of the girls had found themselves in a world of trouble before Roz had found them and given them a way out, hope, family and future that most knew they wouldn't have without her.

After calming her boss down, Evelyn had requested a new go-bag be delivered. They arranged for it to be left in a locker at the car hire place in Courchevel 1850. She agreed to contact her when she got to Paris.

Alex had called Jack and after a much briefer conversation which she hadn't heard, had declared they were moving to his private residence in Paris. Evelyn had baulked at his telling her what to do but had eventually conceded. She knew once they were in Paris she could do whatever she wanted, and he wouldn't be able to stop her.

They had arrived in Paris an hour earlier after picking up a car and her new gear which was precisely where Roz said it would be. She and Alex had shared the driving, for her part she had used the time to study the man he had become. Alex had always been jaw-droppingly gorgeous, now he was panty-dropping gorgeous but with the added edge of sex appeal that came from the dangerous vibe that seemed to emanate from him.

He had changed a lot in the fifteen years they had been apart. The softness of the boy had hardened leaving a man who called to her on every level. She knew he had done the same to her—studying her as she drove. Evelyn couldn't help but wonder what he had seen when he looked at her. Her changes were not only on the surface. The girl she had been was gone, buried underneath experiences and memories. Some she wished she could change and others she cherished.

Now Alex was driving, moving through the traffic towards the Left Bank area of the city.

"Where are we going?" she asked as the early morning sun rose over Paris turning the sky a stunning peachy-blush-mauve colour that made Evelyn itch to grab her paint pallet in an attempt to recreate it. The feeling was so foreign it startled her for a second. She hadn't painted in so long she wasn't even sure she could any more.

"We're going to my apartment," Alex replied snapping her from her thoughts as his deep voice caressed over her.

"You live in Paris?" She turned in her seat towards him her interest piqued.

He glanced at her. "Yes, on the Left Bank. Bon Marche to be exact."

His words hit her square in the chest as the air seemed to dissipate from the car.

She knew Alex could see the effect his words had on her as she sucked in a breath.

His voice was gentle as he reached his hand to caress her cheek with a whisper soft touch. "Evelyn."

Evelyn fought the desire to lean into his touch, instead she pulled herself together with an iron will. "Wow, that's fabulous but why are you taking me there?" Evelyn made sure to keep her voice calm despite the emotion swimming through her.

The Left Bank was their dream destination as youngsters. They had lain on the bank of the river near her home and talked about how they would live on the Left Bank. She would paint and he would open a Patisserie close by or open his own restaurant. The fact that Alex had fulfilled a part of his dream hurt more than she'd ever thought possible.

"It is the safest place to lay low until we figure out what's going on." He spoke calmly but with a hint of steel in his voice as if he was ready for her argument.

"Okay," she replied because although she had no intention of staying with Alex it was too painful having her memories raked over wounds she'd thought healed but now she realised were only dormant waiting for the right time to bleed.

"Okay?" He seemed surprised at her capitulation.

"Yes, you're right. It probably is the safest place for now," she said glancing at him.

Alex threw his head back and laughed. It was thick, sexy and so familiar. "You still can't lie to me. No matter how much you might have changed, that hasn't," he said as he pulled into an underground parking garage and killed the engine.

Evelyn frowned and pursed her lips at his hilarity directed at her. "Still so cocky," she snapped. She crossed her arms and glared at him in an unspoken challenge to laugh again.

Alex said nothing but exited the vehicle and moved to her as she did the same. Taking her bag from her which made her scowl at him, he led her to the elevator that was accessed by a thumbprint. The doors slid open and he followed her inside hitting the button for the top floor as he did. Being in an enclosed space with Alex made her feel like she couldn't take a breath without smelling his scent or feeling him close. Her skin prickled with sensation and he wasn't even touching her.

"If I recall," he said softly so close to her ear that she shivered, "you quite liked my cock-y,"

Evelyn was saved from answering by the doors opening on his apartment. Alex stepped past her and Evelyn followed taking in the most beautiful apartment she had ever seen. It was her dream home. The living space was completely open with an L-shaped couch to the left, a glass coffee table in front, and cream area rug which covered the pale oak wood flooring. A further table to the left of the couch held a lamp in matt silver. A floor to ceiling window was beside the couch and an abstract print on the wall separated that from sliding doors which led to a balcony.

Directly in front of her was a glass dining table, and behind that, one wall was taken with sliding glass doors that also led to the balcony. She could imagine sitting there in the summer with the doors completely open enjoying a glass of wine. Evelyn stepped forward and her eyes caught on the right side of the room where an open plan kitchen was set back facing the dining room and living room, units sat between the space with a breakfast bar on top, stools tucked neatly under. She could imagine Alex there cooking while he chatted with friends or a lover.

The wall closest to her on the right before the kitchen was inset with shelves covered in books. Alex had always loved to read, and she was happy to see he had kept up with that. Off from there she could see a hallway that led to what she guessed were the bedrooms and bathroom.

"Wow, Alex, this place is amazing! How long have you lived here?" she asked moving closer to the balcony, her hand skimming over the glass table reverently.

"About four years. I only just finished the renovations. It was a wreck when I bought it. I've been working on it between missions and finally got it back to how I imagined it could be." He looked around and nodded. "I'm pretty pleased with it."

Alex stepped in front of her and slid the balcony door open for her. Stepping out she saw that space had a herb garden in planters and some lavender. It followed a large L shape design, covering the dining room and kitchen aspect and the living room side. The view was breath-taking—curved rooftops in the foreground with the Eiffel Tower in the distance. The sun had risen fully now, and the winter sunshine was glinting off the buildings made everything shimmer.

"Are you hungry?" Alex asked from behind her.

She spun and found herself almost touching his hard chest. Looking up she forced herself not to step back and show him exactly what his proximity did to her. "I could eat but cereal is fine."

Alex looked down his aristocratic nose and raised an eyebrow at her request. "I'll make us something." He turned and moved towards the kitchen. She watched him busy himself opening and closing cupboards. The cold wind moved through the buildings as the winter chill hit her making her shiver.

Walking back inside and sliding the door closed Evelyn moved to the breakfast bar and hitched herself up on a stool. Alex was mixing pancake batter and chopping fresh fruit.

"Can I do anything?"

"No, I can handle pancakes," he said with a grin. "There's a phone over there. He pointed with his chin towards the glass coffee table. "It's secure so if you want to call Roz for an update you can."

"Thanks." Picking up the phone she looked at it for a second. Her instinct was to take it in another room away from prying ears even if they were Alex's ears. *You don't know this Alex!* her mind reminded her, but she felt like she did and that was probably dangerous.

"You can use the bedroom at the end of the hallway if you want privacy," he said as he looked up from pouring batter.

"That's okay. It seems we have the same goals right now," she responded and called Roz on her cell.

"Roz."

"Hey, it's me."

"Evelyn, talk to me," Roz demanded in her usual gruff way.

"I'm with Alex at his place in Paris." She didn't say where, as it wasn't necessary. In any case, if Roz wanted to know she would find out. "Any news on what it is the British Monarchy thinks I have?" She knew Roz would have been working all her contacts to find as much information as she could and wanted to get to the point as she could see Alex plating up. Her stomach was now rumbling as her taste buds salivated.

"We don't, no. The only thing we know is that they think you have something that would cause them great embarrassment, maybe even bring down the Monarchy."

"Is that all?" Evelyn sighed. "Honestly I wish I had whatever it is they think I have. At least I could give it back. Is there any news on Petra Chance, the woman I helped?"

"No. Lili is looking for her. As soon as I know more, I'll contact you but for now stay low and stay safe."

"What about the people who blew up my chalet?" she asked tucking the grief away at the thought of all the memories that had been created there. That chalet had been the first time she had felt safe since she had left Alex and her home.

"We're working on it, but we aren't the only ones. Eidolon is investigating it too. We need to tread carefully. I know you're with Alex and that Jack owes you, but they can't be trusted, Evelyn."

Evelyn felt her tummy knot at Roz's reminder. Her eyes moved to Alex who was the epitome of domestic bliss as he served her breakfast in her dream home in Paris. *Why, oh why, can't this be real?* "I know, Roz. I'll be careful I promise." She disconnected the call.

"Breakfast is served." Alex pulled out a chair for her as if they were on some kind of date. Evelyn ignored it and sat in a chair on the opposite side. She saw him frown but he said nothing as he moved her food across to her before sitting down and tucking into his own.

They ate in silence. Her previous excellent mood was now drooping along with eyes, but Evelyn still enjoyed the fluffy butter-milk pancake and fresh fruit along with the crispy bacon and scrambled eggs. Fresh and fragrant coffee which she knew without a single sip was rich and full of flavour was next to her with cream and milk.

It was perfect and it made her angry that it wasn't real.

She saw Alex push his plate away and sit back in his chair regarding her. "What did she say?" he asked calmly even though she could see the tension in the stiff way he held his head.

"Not a lot. Just what you said really." She held his gaze as she faced him and took a sip of the coffee and realised she was correct —it was terrific coffee.

"Bullshit! Before you spoke to her you were relaxed, now

you're tense and quiet. What did she say?" he demanded pushing himself from the chair and rounding the table to her.

Anger vibrated through Evelyn. Slamming the cup down she stood and faced him, her hands on the table in front of her. "I told you she didn't say a lot," she returned, her temper flaming as she faced him.

"And I told you that you're a sucky liar."

"Fuck you."

"No, Evelyn. Fuck you."

All the breath left her body at the seductive edge in his tone.

CHAPTER SEVEN

ALEX COULD ALMOST TASTE THE SEDUCTIVE NOTES OF DESIRE in the air they were that potent. His body was screaming at him to lay her back across his glass dining table and sate himself on her body. Make her scream his name as she climaxed, driving out every doubt, every single moment of grief that they had suffered.

His hands clenched into fists at his side as he battled not to touch her. Evelyn had always been beautiful but with her temper in full fury she was something else. The silence in the room was interspersed only by the sounds of their breathing.

"Well, *mi nena*, what will it be? Truth or Dare?" His use of his old pet name for her was familiar and comfortable, and surprised him a little with how easily it had fallen from his lips.

He watched as her pupils dilated at his challenge, her desire winning before a switch seemed to flip and her face closed, and she stepped away.

"I'm not playing games with you, Alex. I'm exhausted and I just want to catch a few hours' sleep and then I will get out of your hair," she said letting the tiredness show.

Alex felt like an asshole for pushing her when she had been through so much. "Listen, I'm sorry. It's none of my business what Roz said but I do want to help you. Whatever happened fifteen years ago does not change the fact you are and always will be special to me, so don't think otherwise—okay?"

Her head tilted and a smile flitted around her mouth. "You always were the best of us, Alex. The fact is Roz has a lot of trust issues and doesn't trust you or any of Eidolon. It isn't personal it is just her." She held up a hand as he went to speak. "Let me finish. Roz doesn't trust you but despite our separation I do. I still see the man who stopped his bike to move a frog from the road so it wouldn't get squashed. So, I'm sorry I over-reacted just now. I'm tired and I need some sleep."

His throat tightened as he saw the girl he had loved in the tiredness around her eyes. Evelyn had always tended to lash out if she didn't get her eight hours and even time and age hadn't changed that. "Of course. Let me show you to your room. We can talk later about things." Alex led Evelyn down the hallway and quickly showed her the master bath and the bedroom next to his.

"Is that another bedroom?" She motioned to the closed door at the far end of the hall.

Alex nodded quickly not wanting her to have any interest in that room. "Well, Delphine has made the bed up so you should have everything you need but if not just shout. I probably won't sleep for a while," he said as he stepped away from the door.

"Is Delphine the woman who stocked the fridge?" Evelyn asked and there was an unmistakable tone of jealousy in her voice which made him smother a chuckle.

"Yes. She's a treasure. I don't know what I would do without her," he replied enjoying the way she scrunched her nose up in distaste.

"Oh. I see...I didn't know you had a girlfriend. I should probably go." She moved to go past him.

He touched her arm to stop her a smile creasing his face. "Evelyn, look." He held up his phone showing her the picture of him and his elderly neighbour from Christmas last year. "This Delphine and I last Christmas."

The photo was one of Alex with his arm around Delphine Fournier, his sixty-five-year-old neighbour from downstairs. They were laughing into the camera while her husband took the picture.

"Oh, that's sweet." She handed the phone back.

"Yeah they both are. Delphine and her husband run the Patisserie down the road. They kind of adopted me when I moved in here. She keeps an eye on the place and gets food in when she knows I'll be home, and I do odd jobs for them. Thomas hurt his back a few years ago in an accident so can't do a lot of the little jobs he used to do. This way they help me, I help them, and nobody gets their pride hurt." He looked at her and caught the soft look on her face.

"Yep, he is definitely still there." She smiled and for the first time it reached her eyes. It took his breath away. He felt the sudden need to warn her that he wasn't the man she knew anymore. The things he had done and seen had changed him in such a way he could never go back to being Alex the boy who loved to cook.

"I'm not the sweet boy you once knew, Evelyn," he said as he pushed her hair back from her cheek his fingers skimming the delicate skin there.

She closed her eyes and he could see she was struggling with this as much as he was but there was too much unsaid between them to do what he wanted to do.

"I know that, Alex. We've both changed more than we ever imagined possible but deep down in your heart where only love lives, you are the same." He knew she left something unspoken but didn't push her when she pulled away and gently closed the door on him.

He stood for a moment wondering what the hell was happening to him. He felt so conflicted, but one thing was entirely clear was in all the time they had been apart his feelings for Evelyn hadn't waned. Indeed, he felt more for her now than he could ever remember feeling back then. It was terrifying because if the British Monarchy got their way, he would lose her for a second time, and it wasn't something he could survive.

Spinning on his heel he headed back to the kitchen and collected his phone from the counter beside the coffee pot. Moving to the window he hit dial and waited for Jack to pick up. As usual he didn't wait long.

"Jack."

"Hey, give me an update on what the fuck is going on," he said his temper still on a simmer as he thought how close Evelyn had come to getting blown up in that cabin.

Completely unperturbed by his demand Jack told him what he knew. "We know that they were professionals, or you would have tagged them before they started shooting at your ass. Blake, Reid, and Liam took care of them after you left Courchevel, so you won't have any more problems. There were no IDs on any of them which further confirms they were professional. My best guess is paid muscle that somehow had inside knowledge about the cabin. What's even more concerning is that they sent a second team in early. Either somebody knows of your connection to Siren or they really, really want her dead. Or there's a second threat we don't know about."

"Evelyn."

"Sorry?" Jack sounded confused.

"Her name is Evelyn not Siren." He hated hearing that name.

"Fine, whatever. Evelyn tell you why she disappeared yet?"

"No. Not yet but she will." He stepped outside not wanting to risk her hearing him even if she was meant to be asleep.

"We'll find out. It might be linked. Also, we have Mitch tailing Lili and he said she was asking questions about a woman called Petra Chance. We think the two might be linked as there was a woman of that name linked to James Colchester's cousin."

Alex remembered Colchester from when they had provided security for Princess Louisa's christening a few years ago. The threat level had been at an all-time high, so they had been drafted in to support CO14 now known as RaSP or Royal and Specialist Protection, within the London Met.

Colchester was the 17th Duke of Crossley and provided legal counsel to HRH. He was a solid guy, but Alex knew nothing of his cousin.

"That's a pretty tenuous link. Do we have anything else? Like who actually issued the order?" Alex was frustrated at the lack of information.

"It came through the usual channels, but I have a meeting with the Princess Royal's Private Secretary later to see what he knows. In the meantime, keep your head down and keep her alive. I owe her and I pay my debts," Jack said before disconnecting.

Alex's mind was spinning from the last forty-eight hours and he needed a few hours' sleep to clear his head. He didn't go to his room though, the thought of Evelyn in a bed next door was too much temptation for him. Instead, he stretched out on his L-shaped couch facing the hallway and closed his eyes.

HE WOKE with a start several hours later when he heard a noise. His eyes shot open and he saw Evelyn tiptoeing down the hall towards the closed door of the third bedroom. *Shit!*

"Evelyn," he said springing to his feet.

Evelyn stopped short and spun around a guilty look he recognised well on her face.

"I forgot. Which one is the bathroom?"

He quirked an eyebrow at her. "Do I need to remind you about lying to me?" His hands were in his pockets as he strolled towards her.

Evelyn tilted her head and looked sheepish while still looking adorable in a way she had no clue she was doing.

Fuck sake!

"Fine. I was curious," she said when he stopped and watched her, his face a warning that he would indeed make sure she was sorry for lying but in the most pleasurable way.

"And why is that?" he asked as he stepped closer to her.

"Because you're hiding something."

"We all have our secrets, Evelyn, and that is mine—for now anyway. Unless you are willing to share yours with me?"

She shook her head and he fought the disappointment her denial brought.

"Fine. Then let's respect each other's privacy shall we," he asked with a grin." He grinned to take the sting from his words.

"Sure. I'm sorry. It was wrong of me to pry when you have been nothing but kind to me," she said as she stepped back towards her room.

"Why don't I put on some coffee and then update you on what Jack told me?"

"Can I grab a shower first?"

"In the actual bathroom?"

She crossed her arms which pushing her tits up, so they almost spilt from her vest top. "Yes, smartass, the actual bathroom."

"Yeah. There should be towels and whatever you need in there." Pulling his gaze away from her delectable body was hard. *No pun intended.*

"Thanks," she said and turned, leaving him standing in the hallway.

Alex put his hands on his hips and looked at the ceiling,

searching for inspiration on how he would get through this without making a total ass of himself. Deciding the ceiling wasn't going to help him, he headed for the kitchen. This was a job for the expensive coffee he kept for special occasions or occasions when his usual blend just wouldn't cut it.

CHAPTER EIGHT

Evelyn felt contrite. Alex had helped her, opened his home to her, and she had been hell-bent on uncovering his secrets and keeping her own. She didn't like it but what he'd said hit a nerve. It also led to more thoughts that she didn't like.

The hot water ran down her body as she rinsed the shampoo from her hair, the smell of raspberry and mint making her crave chocolate. Allowing herself one more minute to enjoy the shower she finally turned the water off and stepped out grabbing a warm towel from the heated rail on the wall.

His bathroom was mostly white—from the sleek modern bath to the glass corner shower. Black tiles on the wall gave it a classy masculine feel but the downlights made sure it was bright and inviting despite not having an exterior window. Evelyn wondered if he had designed it or if he'd had a woman in his life do it. She instantly went to earlier when she'd thought his neighbour was his girlfriend. The pain it had caused had hit her square in the solar plexus. Pain that almost made it difficult to breathe, followed by relief that was almost more terrifying when he'd said she was his elderly neighbour.

Evelyn was the first to admit that she had never stopped loving Alex. He had been her first love, her first lover and while he was not her last, he was her only love. It wasn't something she had intended but no man had ever come close and she had given up trying in the end. All her energy had been ploughed into staying alive and then helping others.

Her reaction showed that seeing him again and being around him had taught her that her Alex, the man she had loved, was still there and more than that he was now far sexier even sweeter and something else she couldn't quite define. She knew he was still attracted to her. The chemistry between them was off the charts, more so than when they were teenagers. This was an adult attraction that far surpassed what they'd had as kids though their love could not be denied.

If she allowed herself to dream though to let him in, then what would happen if she lost him again? Once was enough to kill her, twice and she couldn't even consider the pain. Plus, she would have to tell him why she'd left and that was a can of worms she didn't want to open, especially with this new threat hanging over her head.

Towelling off she wrapped the smaller towel around her wet hair and pulled on jeans and a long-sleeved ruby red base layer over her black satin bra. A squirt of deodorant and she was dressed. Picking up the wet towel and dumping it in a laundry hamper, Evelyn went to the mirror.

Her face was a little pale from lack of sleep but other than that nobody would know what an exciting few days she'd had. Slathering tinted moisturiser over her skin she added a lick of mascara and pinched her cheeks to give them some colour. Finally, she shoved on warm socks and black, low heeled boots.

Moving from the bathroom she could hear Alex in the kitchen pottering around as she went back to her room. *No. Not my room, the place I'm sleeping.* This was not a permanent arrangement—it was a temporary stay. So why did it already feel more like home than her own house did? Because Alex was there, and he had always been home to her.

Pushing her toiletries back into her bag, Evelyn flipped her head and roughly dried her hair before pulling a brush through the long, black locks. Deciding to leave it down she took one last look in the mirror and decided she would have to do.

Alex was adding meat to a crock-pot when she walked in the kitchen. His head came up and his eyes slid over her from top to toe, appreciation in his eyes before he dropped his gaze back to the counter.

"Coffee?" he asked as he turned to the pot, his movements controlled, and no energy wasted.

"Please," she answered as she." She pulled herself up to sit on the stool at the island opposite where he was now chopping carrots. "So, what did Jack say?" she asked as she sipped the fragrant coffee, the intense smooth flavour hitting her taste buds.

Alex again glanced up as he spoke his fingers a continued blur as he chopped and diced the root vegetables. "They don't know a lot but are following a lead on a woman called Petra Chance. Ring any bells?" His body looked relaxed, but Evelyn knew he was testing her to see if she would lie.

"You know I do, Alex," she replied and watched a content look pass over his face.

"Tell me about her?" he said as he twisted to add the veg to the meat.

"She was dating a man named Simon Booth. He's related to the Duke of Crossley. Petra was in a bar one day and I happened to see them fighting. He was getting physical, grabbing her arm and snarling in her face. I've seen fear and she was scared of him." She took another sip of coffee and noticed a nerve in Alex's jaw was ticking. He was angry but he stayed silent and she continued. "Anyway, when he staggered off to the toilet I went and spoke to her and offered my help. She didn't take it, but I gave her my card. I forgot about it, then she called me out of the blue and asked me to help her get away from him. I helped her get set up in a new place in Bath far away from him and that was it. I kept in touch for a while but haven't heard from her in a few months. That's it." She shrugged her shoulders. "I've asked Roz to check in on her though as she's the only link I have to anyone remotely royal."

"Jack has a meeting with someone today to try and get more answers. The team that blew up your place have been dealt with by Liam, Blake, and Reid so we don't need to worry about them. What is worrying is that they sent someone so quickly on the back of us taking the job. Jack will call as soon as he knows anything though so for now, we wait unless you can think of anything else?" he asked as he moved to the sink and washed his hands drying them absently with a tea towel.

"Not really. Until we know what I'm accused of I can't defend it or figure out which way to go from here. Hopefully Roz or Jack will come through for us." Her eyes were on Alex as he rounded the counter and came to lean his hips against the island beside where she was sitting.

His arms crossed over his chest as he looked at her a quirk on his lips. "So, do you want to hang around here or come meet Delphine and Thomas?" he asked with a tilt of his head and a small smile on his full lips.

Evelyn felt excitement invade her body at his invitation. He was offering her something of himself without asking for anything in return. "I'd love that," she said with barely concealed enthusiasm.

His grin when it came made her heart stutter, but it was his actions that made her belly flip in a way that she wasn't sure if it was pleasure or pain. He stepped into her, his body close but not touching and lifting his hand ran his index finger down her cheek.

"I've missed you, *mi nena*."

Her heart hammered in her chest like she had a run a marathon, every nerve sensitised to the light touch on her face. Evelyn closed her eyes frightened he would see every emotion that was coursing through her. The desire to lean into it almost got the better of her before he dropped his hand.

"Me too, Alex," she whispered as he walked away not hearing her words.

Taking a second to compose herself Evelyn took a deep lungful of oxygen before she followed and a feeling of lightness that was at odds with her current situation settled in her soul.

———

DELPHINE AND THOMAS were a delight and the patisserie was everything a French patisserie should be. Welcoming her with open arms they seemed to know who she was. Their eyes had gone wide when they saw her before flashing to Alex in question. Alex had made the introductions and they had been warm and friendly in their greeting.

Looking around the sights and smells were making her mouth water. Lemon tarts, raspberry tarts, macaroons of every colour and flavour, caramel mille-feuilles, and eclairs like she had never seen. Pistachio, praline and nougat, raspberry—the variety of eclairs went on and on.

The shop was divided into two with sweets and desserts on one side and loaves of bread on the other. Directly opposite the entrance was a counter that sold coffee, hot chocolate, and tea. Six or so tables and chairs were dotted around, with low comfortable chairs around coffee tables in the windows.

They were led to the back and a table and chairs where Delphine took their orders. "Alex, my sweet boy what can we get you and your lady?" she asked her French accent strong with excitement as she laid smiling eyes on Evelyn.

"I'll have a hot chocolate and one of your Rum Babas." His warm smile spoke of the affection between them.

"That sounds good. I'll have the same," Evelyn said with a smaller but still friendly smile.

She watched as Delphine bustled off to get their drinks and cakes before turning her attention to Alex who she noted was already watching her. "They are lovely people," she said softly.

"Yeah they are." He glanced at them. "When pop died four years ago, I took it hard. They were there for me and filled a void that I hadn't known was left," he said with a frankness that startled Evelyn. The revelation that Alex had lost his father hit her hard.

"I'm so sorry, Alex. I didn't know," she whispered over the lump in her throat.

Mr Martinez had always been sweet to her. A quiet man with a big heart and quick wit he had always made her feel like she was family right from the day she had met him until the last time she had seen him. A carpenter by trade, he had made her a small wooden jewellery box for her sixteenth birthday. The detail and exquisite mastery turned it from a simple box into something of exceptional beauty. She had treasured it and she wondered sadly what had happened to it.

"You couldn't have known I don't suppose," he said, and she could tell by his tone that he wondered if she could have.

Maybe he did put some blame at her door, and he would be right, but it was done, and she couldn't change that.

"Alex," she started but Delphine arrived with their cake and drinks and interrupted what she was about to say.

"Two hot chocolates and two Rum Babas," she said placing them on the table between them.

Evelyn tore her eyes from the guarded look in Alex's eyes and smiled although she knew it didn't reach her eyes. "Thank you! These look delicious."

Delphine practically beamed under her praise. "My Thomas,

he is the best pastry chef in France." Her pride and love for her husband shone through her voice. The look she shot him over her shoulder as he looked at her with so much love made her feel as if she was intruding on something private.

"Delphine, I thought you said I was?" Alex said with an affectionate wink at the older woman that made Evelyn jealous that it was not aimed at her.

She realised with a jolt that she had missed the warmth and security she had felt from being in his orbit. He had a way with him that made people comfortable and he wasn't afraid to show he cared, never had been. She thanked God he hadn't lost that.

"Now, my Alex, you are second best," Delphine said on a laugh as she placed her hand on Alex's shoulder.

Evelyn watched as he put his hand on hers and squeezed gently. "Okay, Delphine, second to Thomas is good enough for me,"

"I leave you now. Enjoy." She dropped a kiss on Alex's cheek and headed to another table.

The air was stilted, and she had no idea what to say. For so long she had been confident wearing her persona of Siren, never having a situation out of her control and yet now Alex was peeling back the façade leaving her exposed and she felt vulnerable and yet safe. How could one man illicit so many feelings at once? She was pondering this while she took a bite of the Rum Baba and then the thought was gone as she had a climax of the taste buds. The groan left her mouth involuntarily as the sweet taste hit her.

"Oh my God," she groaned, and her eyes rolled back in her head.

The thick bark of laughter from Alex made her open her eyes and see him with his head thrown back, the arch of his throat in her vision, the sexy curve of his Adam's apple the luxurious warmth of his humour and then he looked at her and all the air left her in a whoosh.

She was still as in love with him now as she was the day she left him, and he would probably never forgive her when he found out why she had left. Why she had walked away of her own free will leaving a hole in his heart as big as the one left in hers.

His hazel eyes seemed to darken with desire and something else. She knew the time was coming when he would demand answers to the questions she could see in his eyes. Answers that he deserved but ones she was not sure she could give him.

"Still my sweet Evelyn and yet not," he murmured as he sipped his hot chocolate.

"I'm not sure I was ever sweet," she replied taking a sip of the sweet chocolatey liquid before licking her lips nervously.

Alex drew in a breath as his eyes followed her tongue before abruptly standing and hauling her from her seat. "Time to go," he said with an authority that made her body liquify just as her heart began to pound.

It was time to pay the piper!

CHAPTER NINE

As Alex dragged a somewhat stunned Evelyn behind him through the quiet street of Bon Marche, he had exactly one thing on his mind. To get her home, make her talk, and then fuck her until she didn't have the strength to leave him again. His plan was thwarted about five hundred yards from his doorstep when his phone rang followed two seconds later by Evelyn's phone going off.

It could either be very good or very bad, but one thing was clear, it was an interruption he could not ignore. No matter how much his body wanted him to. Keeping hold of her hand even as she tried to pull it away, he took out his phone and noted it was Jack. Deciding to call him back once they were inside and off the street, he hit ignore and watched as Evelyn did the same.

They rode the elevator in silence, her hand tucked in his, their bodies only a breath apart. The tiny space filled with the sexual tension radiating from them. The door opened and he stepped out, pulling her into his front, so her breasts were plastered against his chest. His hand lifted and sifted through her hair to cradle her nape as his thumb caressed her jaw.

"This is happening," he said, then slanted his mouth over hers in a kiss that held passion, anger, and a sweetness he hadn't expected. She didn't fight him but kissed him back, her hand moving over his chest and into his hair as she gave him everything he needed. Hearing his phone ring again he reluctantly pulled away, the sweet taste of her still on his lips as he held her hooded eyes with his own and answered the call without breaking eye contact.

"Yes?"

"Where the fuck have you been and why the hell didn't you answer your phone?" Jack demanded, the urgency in his tone suggesting something had happened.

"I took Evelyn to see some friends," he responded as calmly as he could considering his body was still thinking about the filthy things he wanted to do to the woman in front of him.

"This isn't a fucking jolly. We have serious problems. If you want a day trip with friends, do it another time."

"Tell me," Alex demanded.

He could hear Jack take a deep calming breath before he spoke again. "My source tells me they believe Evelyn has taken a file that contains evidence about Princess Caitlin. They don't want it getting into the public domain."

"Shit! I take she isn't the Queen's granddaughter?" Alex guessed.

For the Palace to be after Evelyn like they were, it had to be something bad. A princess that wasn't really a princess was as bad as it got.

"They wouldn't say, but they want it back and they want Evelyn gone. I did manage to convince them that we believe there's been a misunderstanding and they have agreed if it's returned and Ms Garcia hands herself in for questioning, they will consider the matter closed."

"You and I both know that's bullshit. If they think Evelyn

knows something she might go in for questioning, but she won't come out. At least not alive." He saw Evelyn wince at his words and cursed his bluntness then for speaking aloud.

"I know, so we need to find out who really stole it and why they are setting up Evelyn."

"Any other leads?" Alex asked and twisted towards the window letting go of Evelyn when her phone rang.

"No, but I'm waiting on a call from Mitch. You need to do some digging and establish every enemy she has. There must be something in her background we can't find. There's an entire five-year period where Evelyn Garcia is missing from every database known to man. I have Will helping us out. He's hacking some of the alphabet agencies to see if he can find her."

"Okay. Call me when you have something."

"Yeah, yeah and answer your fucking phone next time." Jack said and hung up.

Alex turned to see Evelyn had walked towards the window but was murmuring on her phone with her head bent as she tucked her free hand in her pocket. He needed to force her to open up and tell him why she had disappeared. It was all linked, he was sure of it.

Just as he was about to step towards her the glint of a lens bounced off the early afternoon light across the road. He had a split second to shout a warning as he dove across the room at her and tackled her to the ground as a bullet hit the glass of his doors and pinged off.

Rolling off her he saw the shocked look on her face turn to fury as she looked at his sliding doors.

"Bulletproof," he stated as he grabbed her hand and pulled her to her feet, dragging her to the hallway where there were no windows. "Follow me." He walked to the end of the hallway and what should be the linen cupboard but contained his gun safe.

Using the thumb on his right hand he unlocked it and handed her a Colt AR-15 semi-automatic and two cartridges.

He picked up his favoured C8 CQB with flash suppressor and tucked a Glock 17 into his jeans before heading back to the living room. "We need to stay here. This place is a fortress, but I want you fully loaded just in case."

"We can't just leave them out there!" The affront on her face at the suggestion they hide caused his lips to twitch. Despite being under attack he could still hear her attitude and sweet anger, making him smile despite himself. "Alex," she demanded, a frown on her face.

"I have no intention of leaving them anywhere. Liam, Blake, and Reid are covering us so any second now they will..." His voice trailed off as he cocked his ear hearing return gunfire coming from outside.

Within moments silence rent the air and Alex waited a few more minutes before his phone rang. He slid the call button and put it to his ear as he watched an expectant Evelyn. "Alex."

"Tango's are down. Two dead, one alive. What do you want to do with them?" Liam asked his cockney twang for once subdued.

"I'll put a call into Jack for a clean-up team but take the live one to the garages. I want a word with him."

"It's a chick," Liam replied.

Alex buried his surprise at that piece of news. "Makes no difference to me," he growled and hung up. Instantly he called Jack who promised to have a clean-up crew to them within the hour.

He looked down at Evelyn who was now tapping her foot, her arms crossed as she glared at him eyebrow cocked.

"Well?"

"All secure. Two men dead and one woman alive."

"A woman?"

"Yes. I was going down to talk to her now. Are you coming?"

He already knew the answer. Evelyn had never been one to get left behind, not then and apparently not now either.

"Yes, I am," she replied trying to hand him back the weapons.

"Keep hold of them. We don't know what we're facing."

"When did you become such a boy scout?" she teased, her nose wrinkling and reminding him of better times. Times when she was his and they had their entire future planned and it didn't include getting shot at.

"When the woman I loved disappeared." His voice harsher than he intended, Alex saw her face pale at his words. The blow he had delivered seemed to cause her pain as she sucked in a breath. He cursed inwardly at his inept response to her teasing. He wasn't even sure why he had snapped at her. All he knew was he was angry and hurt and he'd lashed out like a two-year-old having a tantrum.

He saw her face close down as she locked her emotions away trying to hide how much his words had hurt her and failing. She had never been able to lie to him or so he had thought.

"Shall we go?" she asked as she moved towards the elevator.

Alex nodded knowing that now was not the time to apologise. Evelyn was angry and hurt now as well, and if he spoke, he would make things ten times worse.

———

EVELYN TRIED to ignore the stricken feeling Alex's words had caused. Her guard had been down, and she had allowed herself to fall into a relaxed teasing place with him. She had known she'd hurt him, but she hadn't realised how much or that he was still hurting. She deserved every ounce of his anger. That wasn't what hurt, it was the fact he had said *had loved*. As in past tense.

She was an idiot to believe it could be any other way. Just because she had never stopped loving him didn't mean he still loved her. Alex had a big heart and to think he hadn't shared it with anyone else was foolish.

The doors opened and they stepped into the freezing cold underground garages to see Liam standing guard over a woman. Blake and Reid were guarding the exits, weapons in their hands, bodies poised as if waiting. Alert energy pervaded the underground garage where they had left their car earlier.

Her eyes took everything in as she zeroed in on the woman kneeling on the ground. Her head was bowed but not because she was injured, because she refused to look at them. She was slim but tall her head coming to Evelyn's chest even knelt. Her dark brown hair was pulled back in a low bun.

"Has she spoken?" Alex asked Liam from beside her as she shivered in the cold air.

"Not a word."

Evelyn watched as Alex approached the woman, his demeanour was calm non-threatening. He was entirely in control and hot as hell. He stopped a few feet in front of the woman far enough out of reach if she attacked him, but close enough to read her intentions.

"Look at me," he commanded his tone direct.

The woman looked up, her eyes moving from Alex to her and back in a slow movement packed full of hatred and anger. Whatever this was it was personal. No operator let that amount of anger show, not for a job.

Evelyn searched her memory for the face and came up empty. She was attractive in a cool kind of way. Probably in her early forties or late thirties if her guess was any good.

"Who are you?"

"My name is Michaela Kirk." The way she spat the words it was clear her name should have some meaning to them. It had none for her, so she looked at Alex and Liam and saw no reaction. Not that they would show one.

"Should that mean something to me?" Alex asked his voice cooler than before.

Her eyes moved back to him and she immediately knew the name *had* meant something to him.

"You murdered my brother," she hissed.

Evelyn caught the slight accent she had up until then kept hidden. Italian if she wasn't mistaken and not middle class. Definitely upper class.

"I have no idea who your brother is," Alex replied and nodded to Liam before turning and walking away.

Evelyn spun to follow him when the woman called out.

"What will happen to me now?" she said as she struggled against Liam who was pulling her to her feet.

Alex stopped and slowly turned. "You will be detained and questioned. Once we have the answers we need, you will be charged with attempted murder." He turned back towards the elevator ignoring the woman's screams demanding to be set free.

Evelyn followed not at all sure what had just happened but feeling reasonably sure it was nothing to do with her current situation.

She waited until they were back inside Alex's comfortable living room before she spoke. "Past mission?" she asked placing the weapon he had given her on the coffee table. The stark black assault rifles looked so out of place in the homeliness of the living space.

"Yeah, something like that. I can't talk about it as I'm sure you can understand." His voice had lost the previous coolness but still remained guarded.

She lifted her hair back from her face with her fingers. "Of course. Are we likely to have any more attempts like that?"

Alex watched her, his eyes going warm and tender before he shut it down. His voice was soft when he answered. "I need to call Jack but afterwards we need to talk, *mi nena*."

Evelyn nodded, her belly fluttering at his endearment. It wasn't the first time he had called her that since they had connected again, but it was the first time he had said it with the warm look in his eyes. "Okay," she replied watching as he disappeared down the hallway and into the locked room she was not allowed in.

Moving to the kitchen, Evelyn rooted through the cupboards until she found a tall glass and then poured herself a cold glass of water. Leaning back against the unit she took a long refreshing drink and sighed.

She knew it was coming but she didn't see how she could come out of this looking good. She didn't want Alex to hate her, but she had to tell him the truth. She owed him that much at least. Holding the cold glass to her forehead she let the tension go and listened for his return. The room was silent, but she felt the exact moment he walked into the room.

Raising her eyes, she saw him watching her from across the room. His body taught; tension radiated off him. Her anxiety skyrocketed. The look on his face told her something terrible had happened.

"What is it?" she asked placing the glass on the side and moving to him her hands gripping his tee-shirt as she reached him.

"I'm sorry, *mi nena,* but Petra Chance was found murdered in her flat." His pause let her know he wasn't done with the bad news.

"And?" she asked her grip on him tightening even as he placed his hands on her hips to steady her.

"Lili was injured. It looks like she disturbed the attacker and was stabbed in the process." His grip on her tightened when she flinched. "She's in surgery now."

"How? Why didn't Roz call me?"

"Not sure. Mitch found her which is how we know."

"Jesus Christ," she murmured as he led her to the couch.

He sat beside her and settled her against his side, and she let him, needing his support. Her guilt at not keeping a better eye on Petra was fighting with her worry for Lili. They weren't that close, not like she and Astrid were, but they had watched each other's backs and she liked her.

Her head came to rest on Alex's chest. The feeling of safety and security made her burrow deeper into him until his scent surrounded her and all she could think of was him. How he felt, how he sounded, the way his skin smelled and tasted.

The muscle was hard beneath her hand as she laid it on his left pectoral, her head resting against his shoulder as his arm came around her holding her, encompassing her in warmth. Evelyn's heartbeat increased as her hand roamed over the muscle under her fingers, feeling it bunch and ripple as he moved.

"Evelyn?" he asked, his voice hoarse with a warning.

"Hmmm?" Evelyn turned her body further into him not wanting to think what her life had become, all the regrets she had, aching to feel him touch her. Her eyes met his when he squeezed her, getting her attention.

"What are you doing, *mi nena?*"

"I just want to feel close to you." Her voice was whisper soft and she saw the desire swirling in his eyes.

Alex lifted his hand and used his finger to lift her chin when she dropped her eyes away. "There is nothing I want more than to feel your sweet body beneath me, to taste you, but not like this. When I fuck you, it will be because it's all we can think about, not because you want to push away the bad," he said as he looked into her eyes. He didn't let her look away even when tears pricked her eyes. "I know I hurt you earlier. I'm sorry. I was cruel and spiteful, and it won't happen again."

"Why didn't you become a chef, Alex?" she asked knowing her question had taken him off guard. It had been bugging her for a while. He was clearly excellent at what he did but she had never envisioned this for him.

She watched as he took a large inhale before speaking. "It felt wrong to do it without you. I lost my love for it. In some ways I blamed my desire to be a chef for what happened. If I hadn't wanted to go to Paris, I would have been with you and we would never have been apart. I decided to join the army instead. It turned out I had an affinity for it, and I won't lie, I loved it. It allowed me to channel my grief and anger in a healthy way. When I was twenty-four, I applied for Delta and got in. That was how I met Jack. We did a joint operation with twenty-two SAS and he was the lead. We got on well and he saved my life when he stopped me from using an entry point which was rigged with explosives. He later offered me a job with Eidolon. The rest is history."

Evelyn shivered at the thought of losing Alex and pondered what he said silently realising how much that one night had rippled out to affect so many people. "What was your unit in Delta?"

"D Squadron. We were primarily assault and infiltration."

"Why did you leave and join Eidolon?"

Alex shrugged. "I wanted the freedom, less politics and more action. I hated the fact we were so stifled by politicians and Jack offered me that. Plus, he's a top operator and I respect him a lot." Alex moved then and dropped a heart-stopping sweet kiss on her nose and then her eyelids before smiling. "Now, how about I whip your ass at a game of Scabby Queen while we wait for news?"

The card game was one they had played often, and she had always beaten him when they were younger. At the memory Evelyn threw back her head and burst out laughing. "Prepare to be beaten, Martinez," she warned as she pulled away feeling lighter and happier than she had a few moments ago.

That was the Alex Martinez effect.

CHAPTER TEN

As he lay on his back in his enormous king sized bed, hands tucked behind his head, sheet pulled just over his hips, Alex replayed the day's events in his head. Taking Evelyn to meet Delphine and Thomas had been something he'd hoped for but never really believed would happen. He had seen the light touch Delphine's eyes when he'd introduced Evelyn.

He had told the older couple about the woman he had loved—still loved—and lost a few years ago when he had got roaring drunk and spilt his guts to them. Delphine mothered him having lost her only son when he was a teen. He let her, knowing the pain of loss well although he couldn't comprehend losing a child. Seeing the light come into Evelyn's eyes as she had taken in the Patisserie had made his chest ache for all the smiles he had missed. Hearing the moans of ecstasy coming from her when she tasted the Rum Baba was too much and the desire to kiss her to swallow those moans, to taste the sweet treat on her tongue, had hit him like a wall of heat. Seeing the same look of desire in Evelyn's eyes he had reacted, not thinking about the future nor caring about the past.

The damn call from Jack had woken him up, made him see

that he needed to take his time with this. He wasn't playing for a quick fuck with Evelyn—he was playing for keeps. But first he had to figure out how to get her to open up to him. Damn attacks from gun-wielding sisters of past missions didn't fucking help.

Alex knew that Michaela finding them was bad. He had indeed killed her brother—child trafficking piece of scum that he was. The mission had been last summer. It had been to break up a smuggling ring that was removing kidnapped children from immigration camps. They then sold them to sick individuals who did heinous things to them before they likely ended up dead in a shallow grave.

So yes, he had shot Jonathan Kirk and he would do it again in a heartbeat. That didn't mean that every life he took didn't steal a tiny bit of his soul—his peace he realised. It took a small bit of his inner peace from him. So even when he was happy and carefree, content even, low down in the pit of his stomach was a knot of tension that dug at him like a burr.

Pushing that thought aside he concentrated on the conversation with Jack. Michaela finding them meant that someone knew where they were. The only way that could happen was if they had a leak. Alex had flat out refused to consider it but had realised to his dismay they were right after a long conversation with Jack and Will earlier. They worked so low in the underbelly of Black Ops that nobody was even sure they were real. Michaela finding his private residence could only mean one thing. Jack was right—they had a leak.

Glancing at the clock he saw it read 01:00 but his body was wide awake. The apartment was silent as he turned his thoughts to the woman who had been the focus of his dreams and sometimes even his nightmares for almost his entire life and sighed. Lili at least was going to be okay. Roz had called Evelyn after she'd beaten him at their fifth game of Scabby Queen.

His lips tipped into a smile at the smug and ridiculously cute look she had given him before helping him finish the dumplings for the Irish Stew he had been cooking in the crock-pot all day. She'd marvelled at his kitchen, even relaxed enough to tease him about being precious over his kitchen knives. That had surprised him especially as he had been a complete asshole and hurt her with his comment about her leaving him.

Alex froze, his body locking as he listened to what he thought was the cry of a wounded animal. In less than a second, he was on his feet and running in just his boxer shorts towards Evelyn's room as the cry became a scream that tore his heart to shreds.

Slamming open the door he saw Evelyn lying in the middle of the bed. Her body curled in a foetal position as her legs kicked at an invisible attacker. Her screams mixed with whimpers made bile churn through his gut.

He moved to the bed, pulling her to him so that she was cradled against his chest. She fought him, her screams becoming louder but he held on.

"Evelyn, it's me it's Alex. Wake up for me, baby, please," he whispered as he settled himself on the bed against the headboard, her body across him, her ass in his lap. Her screams eased a little turning into gut-wrenching whimpers.

"*Mi nena*, come back to me. I have you. I have you." He repeated the words over and over until her whimpers became silent, bone wracking sobs. Her tears soaked his skin as he rocked her, holding her safe, promising her he would keep her safe until her body gave one last shudder and stilled. Her breathing evened but he knew she was awake. He had sat with Evelyn so many times and the memory came rushing back to him. How she would snuggle her head under his chin like she was now, her knees bent and leaning towards him. The scent of her hair tickling his nose. So many things were the same and yet everything was different, and those changes almost broke him.

He wanted to rage, to pound the person who had caused his

Evelyn to know this kind of fear. But he couldn't so he held her and did what he could to give her some peace in a world where there was so very little of that.

How long they lay like that he didn't know but after a while she looked at him. He felt his body tense as if some animal instinct in him knew that the blow that she was about to deliver would leave him wounded and bleeding.

Her voice was almost a whisper, the sound scratchy from the screaming and the tears as she started to speak. "The weekend you went to Paris to secure digs," she began, "I was missing you like crazy. Nothing felt the same without you. The sun wasn't as bright, and I had a dull ache in my heart all day from not hearing your voice."

His instinct was right, this was killing him already and she had only just begun. "*Mi nena,* you don't have to tell me." He couldn't bear the pain he heard in her voice. Suddenly the need to know didn't seem important anymore. All he needed was to ease her pain.

"No, please. I need to get this out." Her voice was stronger as her head lifted. Her eyes met his in a look so full of pain and quiet determination that he knew he would endure whatever he had to.

"Okay, Evelyn," he replied kissing her forehead.

Evelyn settled against him again. He mourned the loss of her eyes on him but understood she needed to do this her way. He squeezed her gently to tell her to go on.

"I went down to our river. I always felt close to you there in our place. The place where all our happy things happened. I stayed for about two hours before I heard a car pull up to the bridge."

He remembered how they would lay a blanket under the bank of the small bridge and lie there for hours. She would read and he would listen to her sweet voice wondering what he had done to make him so lucky that she loved him.

"It was dark and late, so I stayed quiet and out of sight. I heard the engine stop and two car doors slam. Two men were talking in hushed whispers then I heard a boot close. I knew deep down... I knew it wasn't good, so I stayed silent but peeked out to see what was happening. I saw two men lift something heavy over the railing and then it splashed into the river. I was frozen. I had no idea what to do. I almost screamed when the second louder splash came. Then they walked away, and I heard the two car doors shut before the car started and they drove away."

Alex was afraid to ask the question that was on the tip of his tongue and she didn't make him.

"I waited for about twenty minutes and then waded into the water and pulled the object to the bank. I think even then my hindbrain knew what I would find." Her voice had gone low and Alex could hear the fear that even now gripped her as if she had been pulled back to that time.

"Anyway, I pulled at the plastic and tape until it came away. What I saw will haunt me every day until I die. A little girl was inside. God, Alex, her eyes were wide open and unseeing. Her blonde hair was matted to the side of her head with blood and her mouth, her sweet cupids bow mouth, was wide open as if she'd been surprised when it happened."

Alex held her tighter his jaw clenched hard as she dragged in a shuddering breath. He was struggling to keep himself together at the pain in her voice.

"I ran all the way to the police station. I was running so fast I nearly ran into someone. A man that saved me. He was a detective, standing outside having a smoke. He asked what was wrong and I told him. He wouldn't let me into the police station, said there were men inside who would hurt me. He took me straight to a safe house and had a man from Witsec and the DA's office take my statement there. Within two hours I had seen a dead body and been taken into protective custody. The men I had seen dump the bodies worked for Omar Fuentes."

Alex sucked in a breath as he heard the name of the man who had ruled the Cuban drug trade for almost forty years before his death in jail six years ago.

"I recognised the men from when they had come into the diner where I worked. I was terrified. It turned out the little girl..." Her voice stuttered on the words and Alex squeezed her tighter into him trying to take her pain away. "The little girl and the other body—her mother—were the family of an American politician. Anyway, I was taken away and put into witness protection. I couldn't contact my family, or you, or anyone. I was so torn, Alex. They said that if I didn't testify, they would go free.

"All I kept seeing was that little girl's dead eyes. She was so beautiful had so much life ahead of her. I couldn't let that go unpunished. So, I agreed. It wasn't an easy decision. I missed my family so much, but you...I mourned you until it almost killed me. It felt like you had died, and it was my fault, I should have just run and said nothing."

Alex set Evelyn from him on the bed and her eyes moved to him, fear and anguish in their depths. Sliding an arm around her back he rolled so that she was laying almost beneath him and looked at her. Her eyes slipped away from him and closed.

"Evelyn, look at me," he demanded in a voice barely concealing his anger and surging emotions. Not anger at her, fury at the man that had put her in this position. Her eyes opened and she looked at him.

"This was not your fault. You did the only thing you could. You got justice for a little girl who didn't deserve to die. In the same position I hope I would have done the same thing. I don't like that I lost you or how. Not being there for you when you needed me cuts me deep, but I'm so proud of you. I always knew you were the best of us, and you proved that by making sure you got that family justice."

"But I didn't! It never went to court. David the detective who found me on the street that night found out there was a leak in the Witsec programme, and we went on the run. He saved my life, but it also meant I could never go to court or come home, or I risked putting everyone in harm's way."

"You did what you thought best. You were a scared teenager who was trying to keep everyone she loved safe while staying alive."

Evelyn slow blinked as a myriad of emotions chased through her eyes before she settled, her hand gripping his forearm that bracketed her on the bed. "Really? You're not angry with me?" she asked still unsure of herself.

The doubt was something Alex didn't like seeing on Evelyn. He was going to see it didn't happen again. "Really, *mi nena*. I am not angry with you. I was but I didn't understand then and was acting like a silly little boy. I understand now." He traced her cheek with his finger and saw her shiver. *Fuck* he wanted to kiss her, and he wasn't going to deny himself either. As he leaned in, she went to speak but he stopped her with his kiss.

Evelyn went still but as his kiss deepened, she melted into him winding her arms up across his chest and into the hair at his nape. He kissed her slow and long his hand never leaving her face as he tried to show her how much he had missed her with just his mouth. Finally, he pulled away. He would not make love to his Evelyn tonight, not in the shadow of so much heartbreak, but he would hold her and make sure the nightmares stayed at bay.

Settling on his back he dragged her front to his side, his arm around her shoulder, her hand resting on his belly. "Go to sleep, *mi nena*. I'll keep you safe tonight." *And every night if I have my way*, but he didn't say that aloud.

"All right, Alex." Alex could feel her settle deeper against him, her body relaxing as she let the pain and anguish of her memories leave her.

Alex lay awake and replayed her words in his head. Grief was like a heavy weight on his chest as he thought of her going through all that alone. If he hadn't wanted to go to Paris to study, he would have been there that night. That was the truth, and everything wouldn't have gone down like it did. No, he didn't blame his Evelyn—he blamed himself for leaving her.

He felt the moment Evelyn drifted into sleep. Her breathing became even, and her body became a heavy blanket over his as her leg lifted, and she settled so that she was half laying on him. They had always lain like this. He had joked he didn't need blankets because he had her. At the thought a strange feeling came over him that he didn't recognise for a second. When he did, he was shocked to realise it was contentment. Something he hadn't felt in fifteen years.

He was home. She had given him back his peace and he was never letting her go ever again.

CHAPTER ELEVEN

EVELYN CAME AWAKE SLOWLY, HER HEAD FOGGY, BUT A WARM comfortable feeling pervaded her body. She knew exactly where she was—nestled into Alex's warm body. She should feel embarrassed. Her body was pressed into his, her leg thrown over his hips pinning his body with her own, but she didn't. It had always been easy with Alex. They shared a connection that was older than they were. It felt as if they had been together in a previous life and finding each other in this one, had just picked up where they left off.

She grinned at her silly thoughts but still couldn't deny them. The way he had comforted her and allowed her to get almost everything out while he'd held her—not interrupting or questioning just letting her tell her story and then forgiving her as if it hadn't cost him—was pure Alex.

She felt his body move beneath her and knew he was awake when he ran a strong hand over her naked thigh.

"Never thought I would have this again." His voice, sexy-hoarse with sleep and feeling, caused her to shiver.

"Me either," she admitted looking into his warm hazel eyes,

the quirk on his lips showing her he was happy. His was tousled even though he couldn't have moved far with her laying on him. His head bent to hers and his mouth touched hers in a soft kiss that had her belly going heavy and her clit start pulsing.

"What happened after you went on the run?"

She had known he would ask. Alex was smart, the smartest man she knew, and he also knew her better than anyone even now. "David," she said. The affection she felt for David wasn't lost on Alex if the way he stilled was anything to go by. "He helped me get settled in the UK. I wanted Paris but he said it was too close to you and I couldn't take the risk." Alex rubbed her thigh in a comforting gesture which was far from comforting.

"I went to college and finished my education and was attending Art School at The University of Arts in London. I was in my final year when they found me again."

His hand stopped moving, his body going preternaturally still under her. "Who found you?"

"Fuentes's men. David warned me and helped me get away. He took me to his chalet in Courchevel and kept me safe," she said wistfully.

"You loved him?"

"Yes, I did, but not like you think. He was a lot older than me. He was almost fifty and became like a father to me. He had lost his family in a skiing accident years before and his job had become everything to him. I reminded him of his daughter."

"What happened to him?"

"He died of bone cancer two years after saving me for the second time. Before he died, he put me in touch with Roz. He wanted me to be able to protect myself and had come into contact with Roz before and knew she would do that. When he died, I trained every day with her until I became Siren. I went back to Miami and killed the two men who had murdered little Ellie—that was the name of the little girl they murdered. Afterwards, I stayed on with Roz because I never wanted anyone else to end up running all the time like I had. Plus, I was damn good at it and it paid well."

"And yet after all that you're still my Evelyn," he murmured as he turned and rolled into her taking her to her back.

She looked up at him cataloguing his handsome features. He really could be on the cover of Vogue with his looks and contemplated what he said and then shook her head. "No, that Evelyn is a ghost."

"No, she isn't. I see her, and I never stopped loving her."

Her breath caught painfully in her throat as her heart seemed to miss a beat. "How can you? You don't even know me now?" She was terrified of letting him see the joy his words brought her, scared to hope he meant it.

"Yes, I do. I know you care too much. I know you still wrinkle your nose when you're uncertain. I know you hurt easily. I may not know everything, but I know what is in here." He tapped her chest above her heart. "I can learn what is in here," he said tapping her temple gently.

"We are different now, Alex. Those kids that had it all planned are gone, we grew up. Both of us headed down paths we never would have chosen because of me." Anger rose with the injustice of it all.

"Not because of you, *mi nena*," he said in a low, dangerous voice.

"Yes, because I was fool enough to hang out by the river that night, poking my nose in, and choosing a dead stranger over you," she said with a catch in her voice.

"That wasn't your fault."

She pushed at his chest, anger flaring when it didn't move. "Of course, it was."

He growled in response. "You're pissing me off now, Evelyn."

"Oh, well, you'll get over it."

They glared at each other and then just like in times past they both burst out laughing.

"You're a pain in my ass." He chuckled as he kissed her, and she let him, loving the tingle that shot through her body at his kiss.

She realised as he pulled back that he had manoeuvred her so that he was lying between her thighs with his hard cock pressed against her. "Seriously, Alex. I don't want you to suddenly realise in a few months or a year that you don't love me still and it was hormones or rose-tinted glasses. I couldn't take that."

"Hormones?"

"Well, yeah."

"I'm not a fourteen-year-old-boy, Evelyn."

Evelyn smiled as he pressed his hardness tighter against her. "Well, I *know* that."

"Listen, *mi nena*. I know this is scary and I know we can't pick up where we left off, but I've loved you since I was six-years-old, and I love you still. If you don't feel the same tell me and I'll walk away when this is over, but I think you do."

"Well, of course I do." She threw up her hands in frustration. "You're cute, sexy, protective, you cook, your home is the shit, and you're you. I never stopped loving you, Alex, not in fifteen years. That doesn't mean we can make it work though."

His grin lit up the room. "You think I'm cute?"

"Oh, you're incorrigible." She smiled back at him, her heart light.

"I know but you love me anyway. How about we make no promises and we get through this hit hanging over you. Then we can talk more about where we go from here?" he asked before quickly adding, "although I have no intention of letting you go. Not now and not ever again. I did it once and it nearly killed me. I won't live without you again, Evelyn."

"You've gotten very bossy in your old age," she replied as her assent.

"Is that a yes?" He buried his head in her neck kissing her there.

"Yes, it's a yes," she breathed.

"Good," he said and then kissed her again.

Their tongues parried, each seeking to explore to diminish the years apart as they explored each other in the hottest make-out session ever.

Suddenly Alex pulled back. "I want to show you something."

He knifed from the bed and pulled her with him, and Evelyn did her very best to avert her eyes from the erection that wasn't hidden in the slightest by his boxer shorts. "Alex, I only have a nightie on, what if someone comes in?" she complained as he dragged her to the door.

He stopped and she crashed into his chest as he turned. "I don't give a fuck. You're beautiful, sexy, and home so you can walk around naked if you want. In fact, I would prefer it." He laughed as she jabbed him in the belly before taking her hand and kissing her palm. "This is your home now, Evelyn, if you want it."

"Okay, baby," she replied her voice soft with the love she felt for this man who had in the space of a few days healed some of the pain she had lived with for the last fifteen years.

He walked out of the bedroom and instead of turning to the kitchen or his room he moved to the locked door.

Her heartbeat sped up and she swallowed the tears that threatened. "Alex, you don't have to..."

He silenced her with a kiss hard and swift to her mouth. "Yes, I do, *mi nena*," he said and unlocked the door opening it wide for her to see as he stepped back and plastered his front to her back. His palm on her belly the only thing holding her up as her knees went weak and her vision blurred with hot tears.

"It's always been you and this room has always been yours," he said softly as he buried his head in her neck.

CHAPTER TWELVE

EVELYN COULD HARDLY BREATHE PAST THE LUMP OF EMOTION lodged in her throat. Her step faltered as she took in the room in front of her. Alex stood behind her, his arm anchoring her to him at the waist.

"Alex," she managed to choke out as she moved inside, pulled by a force stronger than herself. The room was white with huge glass windows bracketing the entire corner of the room. It was light and airy, chasing any shadows away.

In the middle of the room set up on an easel was a blank canvas, new acrylic paints, rags, a palette, and best of all her old brushes. As if in a trance she stroked the canvas with her fingertips, the slightly rough feel of it under her touch waking a long dormant need to create—to express herself in art.

Picking up the brushes she ran the bristles along her palm, the feel of it so familiar.

"I carried you with me every day since I lost you," Alex murmured in her ear.

Turning her head, she lifted her palm to his cheek and leaned into him. "Alex." Tears threatened to break free. She waved a hand to encompass the room. "I can't believe you kept all this, that you did all this."

"I think deep down I knew you would find your way back to me and I wanted you to have a place to paint."

"I don't know if I can. It has been so long," she whispered as she pulled away and turned a full circle in the room.

"Would you like to try?" He cocked his handsome head in question.

At that moment she knew why she had never stopped loving Alex. What they had was beyond any bond that could be broken. He had promised to love her forever and for the first time since she had been swept away into a world that she never wanted to see much less be a part of she felt as if she was home.

Was she a fool to believe what she and Alex had lasted the test of time and separation—maybe. But was she prepared to walk away without trying? That was the big question and if she had been asked a few days ago she would have said yes, that the risk was too significant. But now she remembered the bounty, the love, the joy, and the peace he gave her, and she wasn't sure.

If they couldn't make it past everything that had happened and become a new version of themselves together, would she survive losing him again? She didn't think so but to turn her back on a man that loved her like she now knew Alex did would be the ultimate mistake.

"Evelyn?"

"Yes, I would like to try." A tremulous smile formed on her lips.

Alex smiled hugely and nodded. "How about I go and get breakfast started and you paint for a bit?

"That sounds good."

As he turned to leave, and she called his name. "Alex?"

"Yes?" He swivelled back to her almost stopping her heart with the vision he made.

"Thank you," she said simply because there were no words to express all she felt in that moment.

He offered her a devastating smile and winked. "It was my pleasure."

He left then as she stood staring at the door and she realised all the pain and heartache of the past was worth it if it brought her home. Excitement bubbling in her belly she picked up the paints and began to look through them noticing he had not skimped on colours or quality. Mixing up some primary colours she selected a brush—one of her old ones even though there were also new brushes of every size and shape. Again, Alex had made sure they were all of the highest quality.

Approaching the blank canvas, she stood and looked at it and slowly her imagination started to see things it hadn't seen in so long. Shapes and colours moved through her mind as ideas began to take form.

Alex came up behind her and placed some coffee pastries down on a table in the corner.

"Thought you might need this," he said handing her a hairband.

She smiled a grateful smile and went up on tiptoes and kissed his cheek. "Thank you," she said letting her hand trail over his shirt covered chest.

He grinned and placed his hands in his pockets with a shrug. "No problem. Make sure you eat."

He turned to leave, and she suddenly felt unsure. "Where are you going?"

"I'm going to check in with Jack and then do some work on the computer."

"Okay, maybe I should..."

Alex stopped and walked back to her. Taking her in his arms his hands linked loosely at her lower back he looked down at her. "Evelyn, just relax. I'll contact Jack for an update and make sure I listen for your phone. If it rings, I'll bring it to you. You just do your thing and let me look after you. Please?"

Hearing that he would listen for her phone and tell her if anything pertinent came up Evelyn decided to let herself have these few hours. "Okay." At her agreement he kissed her head and walked away while she admired his ass in his jeans as he did.

Turning back to the canvas she knew exactly what she would paint. Her brush started to move, tentative at first but becoming more confident as the long-buried memory began to emerge. Soon her brush was flying, time forgotten as art took over and she bled her emotions on to the canvas. Halfway through she stopped and surveyed the painting. She was rusty, that was easy to tell but she wasn't as bad as she had thought.

Not wanting Alex to see her unfinished work, she lifted the easel and turned it so he wouldn't see it if he walked in the door. Her back was now to the winter sunlight that poured through the windows. She felt none of the fear or apprehension she usually would if her back was to a potential enemy. She knew Alex had her back and the glass was bulletproof.

THREE HOURS later Alex poked his head around the door and looked at her. She knew her time at the easel was up.

"Jack just called. We have a meeting with a contact in two hours that has information about Simon Booth."

Casting her eye over the canvas once more she regretfully laid her paints down. "Okay. Let me clean up."

He spied the still full breakfast tray and frowned. This had been one of the things they had fought about when they were together as teens. Her failure to remember to eat or drink when she was sucked down the rabbit hole that was her imagination.

"How about I make you a sandwich and then clean up while

you eat and shower. As becoming as that paint spatter is, I'm not sure it gives the correct vibe for this meeting."

His sexy smirk which made her belly flip. "I'm fine. I'm not that hungry."

Alex raised his eyebrow as he placed his hands on his lean hips. He gave her a look which was at once sexy and annoying. This was new the Alex, the man he had grown into in her absence. "You need to eat." His tone was firm and brooked no argument.

"I know my own body, Alex," she replied haughtily but secretly enjoying this side of him.

"And I know that if you don't eat you get migraines."

She could tell by his tone he wasn't going to budge an inch and he was right. She did get migraines if she skipped meals too often. It was sweet all the things he remembered but also annoying. "Fine," she said with a glare, "but don't think this means you can boss me around. I'm a grown woman who has been taking care of herself for a long time. I don't need you telling me what to do." She went to sweep past him wondering why she felt so confrontational suddenly.

A steel arm clamped around her bicep stopping her. "Don't behave like a brat, Evelyn. It doesn't suit you. I'm merely trying to take care of someone who means a great deal to me. If that makes me bossy, then so be it but don't ask me to be something I am not. The old Alex is still there but you'll learn the new Alex, the one that has watched those he loves in pain, will not stand by and watch it happen again."

Evelyn hung her head in shame. "Yes, I'm sorry. I'm just not used to it," she relented and watched as his face softened.

He hauled her against his chest and kissed her hard, his body flush against hers making her shiver. Her skin tingled and her blood roared as he continued to kiss her taking from her while showing with his every touch that he meant to look after her. He pulled away and gazed at her face, his eyes heated with a passion that was burning so hot it was a wonder it didn't scorch her skin.

"Get used to it, *mi nena.*"

She could hear the hoarse arousal in his voice. His words sent a thrill through her and she nodded not trusting her voice. Wanting nothing more than to carry on kissing Alex among other more delicious things than anything else right now.

"Go before I decide I'm the one who's hungry," he growled his deep voice resonating in her every nerve. Seeing the hunger in his eyes and knowing they still had to catch whoever had set her up, Evelyn stepped away. But not before promising herself that she would come back to this place.

CHAPTER THIRTEEN

WALKING INTO THE LOUVRE TWO HOURS LATER EVELYN FELT eyes on her again. At first, she had shaken it off as residual emotion from a day full of surprises albeit good ones this time. Now, however, she wasn't so sure as a chill ran down her spine. The contact had picked the location and she didn't like that either, but Alex had seemed sure that they could trust this man based on a conversation with Jack.

She had spoken with Roz on the way there in the car and she had agreed that the man they were meeting was clean or as clean as anyone could be and reassured her that Lili was fine and holding her own. The one piece of information she had passed on that had proved enlightening was that they had heard rumblings about an auction that was being arranged on the dark web.

There was a lot of buzz about it but the big players were being screened before more information was given to any prospective buyers. At this point they didn't know what was for sale just that it was highly lucrative for someone going by the name of The Countess.

Passing through security Evelyn turned to Alex and watched

his confident stride, again admiring his handsome familiar face and yet wanting to keep looking at him like it was all new. She had shared the details of her call with Roz and he agreed with her that it was probably tied to her kill order from the Palace. They just had to figure out how and why.

Roz was going to work the auction angle and try and secure them an invite, and if not her then probably Pax.

"What do we know about this guy we're meeting?" she asked as they moved around a group of school children on a trip.

"James Colchester is the seventeenth Duke of Crossley. His family have owned Crossley since it was gifted to his four or five times great grandfather by Elizabeth the first in fifteen-sixty. James Colchester is a barrister and legal counsel to HRH. We don't know a lot about him other than he is wealthy beyond measure and he has a different woman on his arm at every event."

"Wow. I think I've met him now you mention it. It was at a Gala at the Met. He was the sponsor."

"Yeah, he's a massive lover of the arts and contributes to charity regularly. He's considered by his peers to be a cold and ruthless man but not a cruel one. If you're in his circle, which is small, then they speak very highly of him. If you're not, he won't give you the time of day," Alex said as they moved towards the Egyptian Antiquities department.

"A wise man. So why is he helping us?"

"Not sure but I guess we're about to find out."

Moving to a bench in front of *The Mummy* they sat and waited. Evelyn knew Blake, Reid, and Liam were inside too and it added a level of comfort as the itch in her neck began again. The thought of something happening here with all these people turned her stomach.

She looked left as she felt someone approach and saw a devastatingly handsome man walking towards them. He was wearing a custom suit in French Navy that was obviously designer, a white shirt, a burgundy paisley tie, and a burgundy handkerchief in his top left pocket. He stood around six-foot-four, had dark almost black hair swept back and slightly long at the collar, and an angular face with a sharp jawline and cheekbones that made her artist mind weep.

He also had a coldness about him that could possibly freeze the Sahara. His eyes locked on her and then flicked to Alex as he sat down beside him dismissing her. "I haven't much time."

His greeting was clipped, and Alex responded in kind. "We won't take up much of it."

"The information you need is here." Colchester handed Alex a thumb drive. "My cousin is not a good man and I suspect if he's involved you should act quickly. He's prone to fits of temper and when that happens nobody is safe from it."

"Why would he target me?" Evelyn intrigued by this man who was such a contradiction.

The man in question looked at her, his cold assessing blue eyes peering into her soul. "You took away his toy." His reply was flat, and she couldn't hear any emotion in his voice.

"His toy?" she asked equally as cold.

"Petra." She could hear the irritation in his voice at having to explain himself.

"Wow," she said for want of a better word and not knowing how to convey her fury that Petra had been lowered to the same level as a piece of plastic used to entertain children.

"Those are not my words, Ms Garcia," he responded in a clipped tone.

"Why are you helping us?"

James Colchester angled his head to look at Alex then looked towards the Art on display as he responded to his question. "I do not want the name of the British Royal Family brought into disrepute by him or anyone else. It is my job to protect them and that is what I am doing by stopping an injustice."

"You're risking a lot to protect them."

"Then you and I have something in common." He stood and looked down at Alex before looking at Evelyn. "It seems both of us would do whatever it takes to protect those we love. I wish you luck." With that final pronouncement he turned on his heel and walked away.

Alex waited for a few moments before standing and offering Evelyn his hand. "Let's get out of here so we can see what we have." Just as he finished speaking a commotion broke out near the entrance to the Mona Lisa exhibit.

Evelyn felt her body tense in preparation as Alex took her hand and dragged her in the opposite direction. Using his comms unit, he told Liam and Blake to check it out and Reid to meet them at the back with a car.

"Shouldn't we see what's happening?" she asked hearing a scream.

Alex looked behind him as he pushed open a door that said Private. "No, it could be a trap." He quickly pushed her in front of him and slid his hand free so he could access his weapon. Will had easily hacked the security and switched off the metal detectors so they could enter the Louvre fully loaded.

"What about the civilians?" Her heartbeat accelerated and her stomach tightened with worry that innocents could be hurt.

Alex stopped suddenly and turned to her gripping her upper arm firmly. "I won't lose you again."

Her tone softened at the expression on his face. "You won't lose me, Alex."

"You don't know that, and I can't risk it. Listen, Liam and Blake can handle it. Let them."

Taking in the resolute urgency in his voice Evelyn relented. "Okay, baby."

She watched as the look in his eyes softened. He regarded her a moment longer as if he wanted to say something but decided against it. "Let's go."

He hustled them through what looked like a hallway that led to staff offices and the kitchens. Seeing a fire door, Evelyn headed for that knowing Alex was behind her watching her back. Stopping for a fraction to listen, she pushed the door open and they found themselves at the back of the Louvre.

Scanning the area, she saw nothing of interest. A few empty vehicles, and a couple walking hand in hand but nobody threatening to shoot them. She watched the end of the road as Reid came around the corner in the black SUV he and the others had used to follow them to the meeting. He was halfway down the block when the red Renault Cleo Alex had driven exploded, throwing the SUV in the air, the force of the blast knocking her and Alex to the ground.

The air around her seemed foggy, the sounds muffled like she was underwater. Her movements were slow as she pushed off her bloody and cut hands to check on Alex who had fallen next to her. He was moving and seemed to regain his senses quicker than she was. He began to stand, wobbling slightly, but he reached for her, his hands running over her as sirens began to sound through the fog.

"Are you okay?" he asked, and she noticed he was bleeding from a cut on his head.

"Yes, but you're hurt!" She lightly touched the cut on the side of his head.

"It's nothing," he said dismissing it like it was an irritation. "We need to see to Reid. Can you stand okay on your own?"

"Yes, I'm fine." Evelyn's eyes moved to the SUV which was on its side behind the burning Cleo. Alex started jogging towards the overturned SUV as he tried to get hold of Liam and Blake on the comms. Evelyn followed closely behind keeping an eye on their surroundings while Alex was distracted. As she stopped beside the vehicle, she could see Reid was unconscious inside and with the strong smell of diesel in the air knew they needed to get him out and quickly. People were running and staggering about looking completely disoriented.

"Can you watch my back while I pull him out?" Alex asked looking at her intently.

"Of course, but hurry. The tank is leaking. We probably don't have much time."

Alex climbed on top of the overturned SUV and tried to pull the door open. After a few tries it gave and Alex leaned in to free Reid who was held in by his seat belt.

Her eyes continued to constantly scan the surroundings looking for a threat of any kind. She would not let anything happen to the two men behind her but especially not Alex. She would, she realised with clarity, lay down her life for him in a heartbeat. More than that, she knew he would do the same for her. Several people started towards her, but she shouted for them to get to safety and after several seconds they did just that. The distant sound of emergency sirens hit her ears and she knew time was running out.

Her instincts went red hot when two black-clothed figures ran around the end of the road. Her arm came out and she lifted her weapon ready to fire if necessary. She saw them slow and then heard Liam call her name.

"Siren, it's us," he shouted as he approached with Blake running beside him.

Evelyn lowered her gun slightly but kept it where she would be quick to react if she needed it for someone else. "Quick. Reid is unconscious and the tank is leaking. Help Alex." She was surprised to hear the slight tremor of fear in her voice. She normally handled pressure far better than that. Blake and Reid moved around her to help their friend.

"He's free but he's a dead weight. I can lift him up to you, but you need to grab him under his arms and pull him free," Alex said quickly.

The sirens were getting closer and Evelyn knew this could be an international nightmare if they were held by the police. Blake leaned in and hauled a bloody Reid from the vehicle before passing him to Liam who gently hefted him over his shoulder. Blake jumped out and Alex followed.

"We need a car!" Blake shouted casting a worried look at Reid.

"There." Evelyn pointed to a silver Volkswagen Touran. They set off towards it with Evelyn leading the way. Taking out a tool kit from her pocket she had the car open in seconds. She smiled at the shocked looks on their faces and opened the door so Liam could lay Reid down.

"Damn, baby, that was hot," Alex whispered in her ear as he climbed in beside her.

She turned to him and frowned. "Me breaking into a car was hot?" She felt a huge grin spread across her face. "How hard did you hit your head?"

"Still a smartass," he returned making her smile as Blake gunned the engine and got them out of there.

Her smile faded as she looked at Reid, the blood on his face mixed with the intricate tattoos at his neck. Someone meant business and she had a bad feeling that all was not as it seemed.

CHAPTER FOURTEEN

OPENING THE DOOR TO HIS APARTMENT, ALEX USHERED LIAM and Blake inside as they supported a very belligerent Reid between them. Reid had come around in the car and although very confused at first seemed to have all his wits about him. He was, however, seriously pissed that he had been blown up.

Locking the door behind them, Alex watched as Evelyn headed to his kitchen to get Reid a glass of water and some pain relief from the cupboard. It gave him an un-adulterated thrill to see her moving around his kitchen as if it were her own. He liked watching her—could do it all day—and needed a to find a way to convince her that they could still make this work.

"Here you go." She handed the glass and the tablets to Reid.

"Thanks, love," he said with a smile that became a grimace when he moved too quickly.

Reid had a concussion and Liam wanted him checked out, but Reid was adamant that he didn't need to be checked. They had argued in the car and eventually Reid had agreed to stay at Alex's place for the night so that they could keep an eye on him.

"Does anyone have any fucking clue how that shit-storm just happened?" Blake asked to the room at large.

"My question exactly," Reid responded with a frown.

"We met with Colchester and he gave us a flash drive. Then as we were leaving, we heard a commotion from the entrance to the Mona Lisa exhibit. Does anyone know what happened there?" Evelyn asked her head tilted in question.

Alex moved closer to her not wanting any distance between them. His heart was still pounding from the adrenalin and fear that he was about to lose her again in a fiery explosion. His front was to her back and he smiled when she leaned her body into his. Sliding an arm around her waist he rested his clasped hands on her lower belly and his chin on her left shoulder noting the way his teammates responded to this new development.

"Some couple were having a domestic and the bloke hit her straight across her face." Blake's snarl indicated what he thought about a man who would hit a woman.

"Set up?" Alex asked.

"Hard to tell, but my guess is yes." Blake still sounded pissed over the incident.

"So, the domestic was a distraction to cause me and Alex to run right where they wanted us too."

Alex could feel her body tense in anger. "I want to see CCTV of this domestic and any CCTV from the road where the car exploded, and I want it yesterday."

"What next?" Liam directed his question to Alex

"I want you and Blake to find out where Colchester is and where he went after the Louvre. I don't believe he's involved but at this point I don't know. I'm going to call Jack and get him to get Will on the CCTV and let him know what happened today. Evelyn, can you go through this file with Reid if he's feeling up to it and find out all we can about Simon Booth?"

"Sure." As she moved out of his arms, a feeling of emptiness invaded him. It was a feeling he didn't much like.

Blake and Liam started walking towards the door, both men keen to catch the bastards that had nearly blown Reid up.

"You want us to clear out the safehouse?" Liam asked.

"Yes. I want us all in one place tonight and then we can decide how to move forward. They seem to be one step ahead of us all the time and I want to know why and how." Alex's mind moved to the conversation he'd had with Jack about them possibly having a mole or traitor within Eidolon.

"Good idea," responded Blake.

Alex watched as Evelyn took off her jacket and noticed the palms of her hands were scraped. In his rush to get away he hadn't noticed them. "Evelyn," he called, and her head came up, her eyes finding his.

"Yes?"

"Come here."

Her forehead wrinkled at his demand. "Why?" she asked instead of doing as he'd ordered.

He sighed and dropped his head looking at his feet before looking up at her again. "Will you just come here, please?" he said catching the grin on Reid's face and wondered if throwing him outside via the window would put him in Evelyn's bad books.

"Fine, bossy boots," she replied and moved closer to him a clear look of irritation on her beautiful face. Reaching him she lifted her head to catch his eyes.

"You're hurt," he stated gently taking her hands and lifting them palm up for him to study.

"It's nothing."

Alex resisted as she tried to pull her hand away and glared at her. "It's *not* nothing. Let me clean it up." He was ready to throw her over his shoulder and drag her to the bathroom if need be.

"Okay, Alex," she said as if she'd suddenly realised he needed to do this for her.

He looked up over her shoulder at Reid who was watching them intently. "Grab yourself some food or coffee. You know where everything is," he said as he walked down the hallway towards the bathroom.

"Cheers, man."

Moving into the bathroom behind Evelyn, Alex closed and locked it. Her eyes went to the lock and then to him. He could see the question in them she hadn't voiced.

"What's going on, Alex?" she murmured.

Alex pushed her to sit on the edge of the bath and before kneeling in front of her taking her hands in his. Snagging the first aid kit he began to clean her palms of dirt and tiny bits of grit as he considered what to tell her.

"Alex?"

He looked up at her beautiful familiar face a face that had been with him in his dreams for so long. Now living breathing miracle in his arms. "I want to tell you something, but it stays between us. No telling Roz or anyone else."

"Okaaaay."

"Promise me, Evelyn," he asked as he wrapped the last hand with gauze to keep the cuts clean.

"I promise, Alex." She lifted her hand to his jaw, his bristles catching the bandage.

"Jack and I think Eidolon has a traitor or mole." He felt and heard her indrawn breath, the surprise at his words evident.

"Who?"

"That's just it, we have no idea. The Kirk woman should never have known we were involved in her brother's takedown. And the meeting today, only Eidolon knew about that meet. So, unless the leak is from Colchester, which wouldn't make sense, then it's someone within Eidolon."

"Wow. I haven't met them all, but I can't imagine any of them betraying Jack."

"I can't either, but someone is." He held her gaze, the gravity of the situation apparent to them both.

"What do you need me to do?" she asked readily as she picked up a clean cotton pad and began to clean the blood from his face.

"Nothing. Just stay alert. If we have a traitor in our midst, we need to be aware of every word, every action."

"Of course," she said as she finished tending to his cut with some Steri-Strips.

Alex looked at the woman in front of him and felt his body tighten. He had thought he loved her before when they'd had their lives planned out. But now, having lived without her and knowing the empty despair of walking through life in a fog of grief, he loved her more. So much it almost made him weak. Loving her made him vulnerable but it also gave him strength and purpose he knew he couldn't live without.

Cupping her jaw with his hand he watched her eyes darken with desire as he tilted his head to hers. Their lips touched, and as it always had with Evelyn, his passion for her ignited like a flash-bang. His body hardened with the need to consume her and to make her his again. Their tongues rallied as her body relaxed into his, a soft whisper from the back of her throat making his cock twitch. Wrenching his mouth away he rested his forehead against hers.

"You have no idea how much I want you. To feel you beneath me, to see your beauty as you come, to hear my name on your lips again but now isn't the time." Regret was etched into every syllable he uttered.

"I know, Alex," she whispered, the warm breath from her words sending a bolt of desire straight to his semi-hard cock.

Reluctantly Alex stood and with Evelyn following behind him

moved back into the living area. Reid was positioned at the island dunking chocolate biscuits in a cup of tea.

"Neanderthal," Alex said with a shake of his head hoping Reid wasn't the traitor. But he had a bond with all the team and couldn't for the life of him see any of them being a traitor. It was that bond that made it so hard to accept one of them was betraying the team.

"Nothing like a good choccie biscuit dunked in tea to ease a concussion," Reid replied with a smirk.

Alex let out a huff not prepared to get into all the reasons why it was so wrong. "I'm going to get the laptop set up for you guys to get the information off this drive while I call Jack," he said heading to his bedroom where he kept his laptop.

Entering the living room a couple of minutes later he saw Evelyn pouring them both a cup of coffee and smiled. Loading the machine, he left it on the dining table before grabbing his coffee and calling Jack. This was one conversation he wanted to have in private.

Alex had known Jack would explode when he heard about what happened, and he wasn't disappointed when Jack answered on the first ring and as expected, hit the roof. "I don't fucking believe this shit. So, either one of my men is definitely a fucking scum bag traitor, or the Queen of fucking England has a snake in her den. Fucking wonderful."

Alex heard him pacing his office and could imagine the scowl on his face.

"That about sums it up," Alex replied unhappily. "Who knew about the meeting?"

"Everyone. I wanted everyone prepped in case we needed to move on something. What about Evelyn?"

Alex stilled. "What about her?"

"Did she call anyone?"

Alex felt his body go solid. "She spoke to Roz on her way to the meet but nothing before that."

"Are you sure?"

"Yes." He could barely get the word out his teeth were clenched so tightly together.

"How?"

"Because I am," he returned not wanting to tell Jack about the art studio he had made for a woman he wasn't even sure he would ever see again.

"But she could have slipped away, made a call without you knowing."

A part of Alex knew why Jack was reluctant to believe his men were behind this, he got it he really did, but he wasn't having Evelyn used as the scapegoat. He would die for his team, but he would sell his soul for the woman he loved. "I'm telling you, Evelyn is not the leak." His calm control seemed to get through to Jack.

"Then we need to find out who it is and fast."

Alex heard the sigh Jack let out and felt for his boss. "Have you spoken to Roz?" Alex knew that while Jack might like Evelyn, he and Roz had a very contentious relationship.

"No, she's ignoring my calls." His frustration with Roz's lack of communication clear through the phone. "Honestly, I have no idea how Kanan hasn't strangled her yet."

Alex ignored the reference to Roz's husband and the state of their marriage, wanting to concentrate on the matter at hand. "I need Will to pull the CCTV from the Louvre and the street where the bomb was planted. Liam and Blake are checking into Colchester. Evelyn and Reid are going through the thumb drive Colchester gave us. Last I heard Roz was trying to find this auction and get Evelyn or one of her girls on the invite list."

"Let me know as soon as you have any intel from the thumb drive," Jack demanded. "I've managed to convince the Palace to let us handle Evelyn and find the secret they don't want exposed to the world. I gave them my personal guarantee that she's not behind this so if she is, it's my balls for the chop! Right now, I'm going to go through everyone's movements with a fine-toothed comb and find that traitorous fuckwit."

"You know, it might be an idea to bring Fortis Security in on this. Zack may be able to look at it objectively and more covertly than us."

Zack Cunningham was the millionaire owner of Fortis Security and an ex-SAS Commander. He and Jack went way back and anybody that knew him and his team, knew they were the best in the business. They had worked side by side with Fortis on a fair few missions and Alex was confident that Zack could be trusted to help them now.

Plus, he was Will's boss and Roz's husband's best friend. He had connections to them but could still maintain a degree of distance.

"Maybe, but with Ava due any day it doesn't seem like the right time."

Zack's wife Ava was indeed due to give birth to their second child any day now and Zack was reportedly driving everyone crazy with his fussing. Alex imagined what he would be like if he was ever lucky enough to see Evelyn heavy with his child and decided that Zack was right—childbirth was terrifying, and planning was everything.

"Well, whatever you decide just know you have my full support."

"Thanks, Alex," Jack replied and hung up.

Alex took a second to school his features not wanting Reid to pick up on anything. For the first time since he'd started at Eidolon, he had to hide from the very people he trusted to have his back and all while trying to keep the woman he loved from being executed.

CHAPTER FIFTEEN

IT HAD BEEN TWO DAYS SINCE THE ATTACK AT THE LOUVRE and they were no further forward. The information James Colchester had given them was substantial. Simon Booth was a fraudster, a womaniser, and an abuser. He was also a narcissistic prick unless she had missed her mark—which she doubted. Evelyn had gotten pretty good at singling out assholes and although she had never met him, she knew from her dealings with poor dead Petra and reading the file he had been born that way. Some people were born evil and others became that way through life and circumstance.

The file had given them a brief history of his family including James Colchester and Simon's various attempts to undermine Colchester and cause as much trouble as he could for the family. He was a prolific social climber and playboy, always wanting to be seen at the most exclusive parties. He seemed to enjoy throwing away his family's money—or more appropriately his trust fund. The fund that was, at their grandfather's behest, run by James.

Twelve months ago, when James had found out Simon was dealing drugs to minors through the private school where he was the governor, James had sought a legal way to have him barred from accessing his inheritance. James and Simon's fight over it had been very public resulting in Colchester banning him from future family events.

Now Simon was linked through pictures—which were also in the file and had been verified by Will as authentic—to some of the worlds shadiest people. His new 'friends' had encouraged him to spread his wings and it seemed Simon was now in the information business.

This all checked out when she contacted Roz. What it did not do was tell them where he was. Throwing herself back in the chair Evelyn sighed. Alex was due back soon after getting a call from Thomas Fournier about a leaky radiator valve. She had met the couple properly yesterday when Delphine had popped around to speak to Alex about his plans for Easter.

Alex had winked at her over Delphine's head as Thomas had rolled his eyes in an affectionate aside. Delphine was really trying to get the dirt on her and Alex. It had been sweet watching Alex with the older couple. He had been patient and answered Delphine's questions about whether Evelyn would be joining them for Easter even though it was months away.

It reminded her of seeing him with his parents and that made her think of her own. It had been so long, and she still missed them every day. She went back every few years to check on them without them knowing. Watching as they grew older and frailer while being so far away—and as far as they knew dead—became harder and harder with every visit.

The door behind her opened and she twisted to see Alex walk in with a smirk on his sexy lips.

"Hey, is everything okay downstairs?" she asked as he slouched down beside her on the sofa.

His long legs stretched out, his arms loose at his sides, he looked at her and nodded. "Yeah, the radiator needed bleeding."

"A handyman as well as an action hero and a chef. Be still my beating heart," she teased, and Alex chuckled.

"Not sure about an action hero." He laughed again as he slid an arm around her waist and pulled her until she was sitting astride him. She went willingly wanting whatever she could get from the man who held her. Her legs were either side of his big thighs and her hands rested on his chest. Alex hadn't kissed her since their mini make-out session in the bathroom the day they had nearly been blown up. She had, however, spent the last two nights in his bed.

With Blake, Reid, and Liam staying under his roof Alex had decided she would sleep beside him. She could have resisted but she didn't want to. Having spent the last fifteen years yearning to be in his arms she wasn't about to deny herself now. And it had been in his arms, as his big warm body curled around her. Her back to his front, legs tangled, she had used his arm as a pillow and slept peacefully. No nightmares, no tossing and turning. Just restful, dreamless sleep.

Liam, Blake, and Reid had headed to meet up with Gunnar in Munich after they had got a tip that Simon Booth's new associates were meeting there. She and Alex were staying there and keeping a low profile as she was still a marked woman.

She felt Alex still underneath her, his body going rigid and glanced at him worriedly. "Alex?" she questioned her head tilted. Worry hit her at the serious almost dark look on his face.

"You still have it." Alex motioned to the pendant that dangled from her neck.

Evelyn's tummy flipped and she cursed her carelessness. Immediately she started to tuck the necklace away inside her jumper where it usually lay out of sight.

Alex grabbed her hand stilling her. "Don't," he demanded pulling her hand away.

Evelyn went to climb off him, but he placed his hands on her thighs stopping her.

"It's nothing, Alex,' she said of the pendant that meant more to her than any other possession on earth.

"It's everything."

Her head dropped and she looked away to the window where snow was falling again.

"Look at me, Evelyn," he ordered, and she twisted her head to his, a gasp almost hitting her lips at the look on his face. It was still serious, but the darkness had moved to something more. It was compelling and beautiful, dark and almost feral in its intensity.

"You still wear my ring."

She couldn't deny it. The hollow circular pendant that had Evelyn Martinez etched on the back with *mi nena* written above, was hanging around her neck. It had been since the day he had put it there, not once had she taken it off. It had been the only thing she had dug her heels in over.

"It was the only thing I had of you except what was in here," she said laying her hand over her heart.

"You still wear my ring," he repeated as he ran his hands along the outside of her thighs moving slowly over her hips until he cupped her waist in his hands.

"Yes, Alex." Her answer was simple because to deny it would be to belittle what they'd had. Fifteen years ago, she had promised to be his forever and, in her heart, she had never broken that promise. She had no idea what the future held for them as a couple or if realistically they even had one. What she did know was that she had become Evelyn Martinez in her heart years ago.

With a growl that Evelyn felt all the way to her clit, Alex wrenched her body to his. Her core was pressed against the hard length of his cock, her breasts pushed against his chest. They were nose to nose as he held still his eyes locked on hers. The swirl of emotion and desire in his hazel eyes holding her captive.

"I want to fuck you hard and fast until neither of us can see straight. Then I want to kiss every inch of you and worship you like you deserve. Make love to you until there are no doubts swirling in your chocolate brown eyes about who you belong too and what we are to one another." She could hear the desire in his husky voice as he spoke.

Evelyn felt lust and need for him curl around her like a vice. Every nerve seeming sensitised to his touch. Her skin burned for him, her heart started to beat faster, her nipples peaked. "Yes."

Before she could finish uttering the single word his mouth crashed down on hers in a kiss so hot, so potent, she knew she would remember it until the day she died. They kissed in a fever of desire. Teeth nipped, tongues tasted, and hands grasped as they tried to touch everywhere at once. The need to feel his heated skin against hers was overwhelming her senses. Alex was everywhere, his hand cupped her breast and she moaned into his mouth at the feel of him touching her.

Alex reared up with her still in his arms and her legs came around him as he cupped her ass and strode towards the hallway. He went past his room and pushed open the door to what she now considered her workroom.

"I've dreamt of fucking you in here so many times over the years." He moved to the old sofa he had put in the room when she had started painting in there, laying her down and kneeling between her legs. Her body, already heightened with desire, flamed with sensation as he covered her body with his. The scent of paint and oil mixed with turpentine but the most intoxicating scent was all Alex.

"I've thought about this a thousand times, dreamt of it," she said as Alex lifted and pulled her top over her head relieving himself of his own.

The vast expanse of tanned muscle that filled her vision made her mouth water. She kissed the heated skin of his pecs as he nipped his way from her throat to her clavicle and down until he was sucking the peaked nipple of her breast into his mouth over her bra.

Heat and wet enveloped her as sensations hit her like a hurricane. Her nails raked down his back as she gripped the denim covered curve of his ass. "Alex," she breathed as he let her nipple go with a pop.

"Tell me what you need baby," he ordered his eyes almost green with desire.

"I want you now. We can do slow later. I want you inside me, now," she said on a husky breath.

She didn't need to ask twice as Alex stood and shed his jeans and boxers as her hungry eyes devoured the hard length of his cock. She had no time to process it though because he lifted her and unsnapping her jeans dragged them down her legs with her underwear in one move. A flick of his wrist and her bra fell down her arms before falling to the floor. Now they were both standing, he plastered himself to her front until their bodies touched head to toe, skin to heated skin, and kissed her in a hard soul-destroying kiss that left her reeling.

Before she could catch her breath, Alex spun her around and sat, pulling her so that she was sitting facing away from him on his lap. "Pass me my wallet from my jeans."

Evelyn bent forward feeling him stroke his hand down her spine and over her ass as she did. She passed the wallet back to him as her body shook with desire, her pussy feeling empty and needy for him. She arched her head back and watched as he rolled a condom over the hard length of his cock. Her body prickled, heat encompassing her at the sight of him ready for her.

"Tuck your legs up," he urged grasping her waist and lifting her.

Evelyn did as he asked planting her knees either side of his hips as she tipped forward.

His big palm on her breast pulling her back so she could feel his front against her spine made her arch with need. The feel of his cock hot and heavy against her thigh had her rising and taking his cock in her hand.

She stroked down with her hand and felt him thrust his hips up into her hand and he swore.

"Fuck me, Evelyn. That feels so good." His one hand left her waist as it moved to the front and found the slick wetness of her pussy. Running a finger through her wetness he plunged it inside, fucking her with it as she stroked him. "So tight and hot," he growled as he rubbed her clit making her moan.

"Alex."

"Right here, *mi nena*," he growled as he kissed her neck.

Alex pressed his thumb against her clit rolling it as his fingers found her G-spot. Evelyn moved against him riding his hand as he fucked her—her climax building until it crashed over her.

"Fuck, Evelyn, I can feel that tight pussy squeezing my fingers. Feels so fucking good baby."

She whimpered as he pulled his fingers out, the aftershocks of her climax ebbing. Before she could miss it though, he drove his cock into her making her groan his name as her body gripped him. The mild sting of pain made it even more intense as he froze, holding her hips still. Evelyn felt full, wanting to move to ease the desperation building inside her again.

"You feel so fucking good, Evelyn. So fucking good. Nothing better in the world than feeling your pussy rippling around me."

"Fuck me, Alex."

Her words were a moan, and he did. He didn't start slow, he fucked her like he said he would, and it was perfect. She knew she would have bruises on her hips from his grip, but she wanted it. To feel marked by her man in a way only she would know. His thumb and forefinger found her nipple and rolled it as he pulled her head around so he could kiss her. The kiss was hard and rough, all the pent up passion they had hidden and denied over the years screaming to the forefront.

"Say my name, Evelyn. Scream my name as you come around my cock," he demanded.

She felt every muscle go electric at his words as he pounded into her soft flesh taking and taking until she screamed, and her orgasm rocked through her as she cried his name.

"Fucking missed this. Ain't ever letting it go again," he said his voice hoarse as his movements became jerky and he came on a whoosh of breath.

For a minute he rocked into her gently before he stilled and pulled her almost liquid body into his wrapping his arms around her. He kissed her head gently and she shivered at the tenderness. She had always loved that about her Alex. He was so gentle with her, but he fucked her like she needed him too, always seeming to know if she wanted sweet and slow or hard and rough.

"I mean it, Evelyn," he said as he squeezed her gently. "I'm never losing you again." He kissed her bare shoulder gently. She hoped that was true but with men out there waiting to kill her he may not have a choice.

CHAPTER SIXTEEN

ALEX STOOD WITH HIS SHOULDER AGAINST THE DOOR JAMB watching the woman he loved more than he had ever thought possible as she painted. They had been living in a blissful bubble this past week. After he had made love to her in this very room everything had seemed to change between them. Neither spoke of the future but they had fallen into a comfortable pattern.

They would spend their days working on leads from either Eidolon or Zenobi trying to track down Booth. He also spent hours trying to figure out who the snake was in the nest that was Eidolon. Later, they would go and spend an hour with Thomas and Delphine. The evenings were his favourite though, he would cook while she painted and then they would fall into bed together where he would make love to her.

He had only found a semblance of what he needed when he joined Eidolon. They were brothers, friends, colleagues. Each one seeking to ease a pain they lived with in some way. To make the world a safer place for innocents. He had done things he wasn't proud of, killed people, tortured them, and each one had taken from him something that he thought he would never get back.

But as he watched Evelyn tilt her head from left to right as she studied the painting she was working on, he knew in his soul it was worth every life he had taken, every punch he had thrown. He would do it all again just to have this moment with her, but a moment was not what he wanted. He wanted it all! He had loved a young Evelyn with a boyish joy not knowing what life could dish out. Trusting that fate had given him his soulmate and they would live out their dreams.

A sneer lifted his lip at the naivete of that young boy. He hadn't had a clue what life was. He wished in some ways he had never found out. He watched the sexy woman who was dressed in nothing but an old, white button-down shirt, her feet bare, her sinful legs naked to the eye, adding colour not only to the painting but to his bland life, and knew he loved her more now than that boy had ever been capable of.

He cherished every smile, every heated look, knowing that some asshole wanted to take it all away from him. He would not let that happen again. He would finish the bastards that wanted her dead. He would rip their fucking heads off, make them wish that they had never uttered her name and then he would give her his name legally, not just on a chain around her neck. On her finger, on her driver's licence. He would marry her and never let her go.

"You gonna stand there all day and ogle me or are you going to come over here and tell me why you're frowning like a grizzly bear?" Evelyn asked making a face that had his dark mood disappearing, leaving only her.

"Ogling you is fun." He prowled towards her.

Evelyn must have seen the look in his eye because her eyes went heavy with desire as she laid the brush down in the turps and moved towards him.

"I can think of more ways to have fun." Her throaty voice made his dick, already semi-hard from just watching her, twitch. She moved into his arms, banding hers around his neck as she flattened her body to his. The hardness of her nipples rubbing over his chest made him growl as he bent and lifted her, her supple legs going around his waist.

"Yeah what's that?" He almost growled when she bit down on his earlobe before sucking it into her hot mouth as she rubbed her body against his making him groan. His body wanted to be buried inside her.

"Scrabble."

She laughed and jumped down causing him to release her in surprise. His mind was still catching up as she giggled and ran from him showing her playful side which was sexier than Siren would ever be to him.

"You little brat. You're going to pay for that," he said and turned to watch as she took off running. He smiled inwardly knowing that it was going to be all the sweeter when he caught up to Evelyn.

He caught her in the kitchen pinning her to the counter as laughter slipped past her lips, lodging in his chest in a way that was so sweet it almost hurt. Her arms came around his neck again pushing her sexy tits against his chest as he rested his hands on her hips, his fingers digging in slightly to her soft flesh.

"You in the mood to play, *mi nena*?"

Mischief ran across her face, the image of the girl he had loved merging with the woman he worshipped. "Hmmm. What did you have in mind?" she asked her voice throaty with desire making his cock harden even more.

Alex lifted her placing her ass on the worktop and stepped between her open legs causing her shirt to ride up and offering the perfect view of her soft supple thighs. He trailed a hand down over her hip, his thumb skimming the edge of the white lace underwear she wore. He watched her shiver at the light touch. He could see the heavy desire in her eyes as he looked at her.

"Well, I thought first I would get you off with my fingers." He slid his finger up the wet slit of her pussy finding her clit and rolling. The harsh inhale of her breath made him grin as he eased a finger inside her hot pussy.

"Um," she moaned as she leaned back giving him more access. "I could definitely get on board with that."

"Then I figured all that work would make me hungry, so I would eat that sweet tasting cunt of yours." He felt her body contract around his finger at his crude words. Evelyn, he had discovered, loved it when he talked dirty.

"Then what?" She moaned as he drove her towards her first climax of the day, her body responding as she rode his fingers, her hips pushing up towards him seeking more as he held her back each time she got close.

"Well, then I want you to suck my cock. Get it nice and wet so I can fuck you on this kitchen island." His body burned with the need to be inside her.

"Yes," she groaned as he slid a second finger inside pushing her higher as her body writhed. She was fucking glorious and her eyes found his as she crashed, her orgasm slamming through her, her body contracting around him. The dark depths of her eyes almost black pools of bliss as she came.

"Fucking beautiful," he growled before withdrawing his fingers and bringing them to his lips, sucking her sweet juices into his mouth as she watched. Before the aftershocks of her climax could subside completely, he went to his knees, hooking his arms around her legs and pulling her to the edge of the counter. Then he did precisely what he said he would and so did Evelyn before he carried her to their bed and fucked her until they both fell into an exhausted but contented sleep wrapped in each other's arms.

THE RINGING of his phone pulled him from a dead sleep, his arm reaching out to grab it from beside the bed before he was even fully awake. He slid the answer button across and felt Evelyn roll into him, her hand rubbing over his pectorals. He looked at her, a grin breaking through as he spoke. "Yeah?" He kept his tone neutral, not wanting to give anything away to a withheld number.

"Alex, it's me."

Alex went still as he heard Jack's voice. On the other side of the bed Evelyn's phone began to ring. His senses came alive, sleep long forgotten as he read Jack's tone and knew there was trouble.

"Talk to me," he said as he saw and heard Evelyn answer her phone.

"We got a lock on Booth."

Alex felt his adrenalin spike. Finally, they could catch this bastard and neutralise the threat to the woman he loved. "Where?"

Evelyn's eyes moved to his at his question, her expression no longer the look of a woman who had been thoroughly fucked. No, she was pure Zenobi now, and she looked every inch the deadly woman she was, and he loved her for it. She had shared every facet of herself with him over the last few weeks. She was not afraid to show him who she was, the multiple layers that made her Siren, Evelyn, and *mi nena*. He winked as he reached his hand to her and she took it as she continued to listen to whoever was on the phone. They would face it together and either come out victorious or go down fighting.

"Monaco, and word is he has the evidence that HRH wants back and is holding an auction on Saturday night. We don't know the location yet though, so I want you both on the private plane within the next two hours. You'll meet Liam, Blake, Reid, and Gunner there." Jack paused. The silence was deafening, and Alex tensed as he waited for the axe to fall.

"Just fucking say it, Jack."

"You have forty-eight hours to stop the sale and retrieve the evidence or the Peers have voted to make you and Evelyn the public scapegoats and put a price on your heads. You'll effectively be hung out to dry and targets put on your back." Alex could hear the barely restrained fury leeching through Jack's words.

"Fuck."

"I'm doing everything I can but if shit goes south every man at Eidolon had voted to stand with you."

"I can't ask you to do that, Jack."

"Fuck off, Alex. You didn't ask, and it isn't up for debate. They hang you out to dry, they hang us all. We're a team and we don't run when someone threatens one of us. We fight, and we fight dirty if we have to. I still have a few things tucked up my sleeve," he replied almost angrily.

"Thank you, Jack." Alex knew anything else would be dismissed.

He got a grunt in response. "Just go do your job, Alex."

The phone went dead, and Alex looked at Evelyn who had concluded her call and was watching him expectantly.

"Jack?"

"Yeah." He nodded as he reached out and cupped her cheek wishing he could lock her away until he had dealt with this. He knew she would never forgive him though, and to deny her this would destroy their new relationship before it began.

"I guess we're off to Monaco then." Her lithe, sexy and very naked body distracted for a second as she stood and moved to the bathroom.

"Yes, let's get this fucker so we can go back to being just normal people," he said as he stood.

The bark of laughter from Evelyn had his head flying up. She was standing in the doorway, her body angled to him making his body respond in a purely primal way and she was laughing loud and deep. It was the most stunning thing he had ever seen.

He walked to her and slipped his arms around her pulling her into his body. "Care to share what is so funny?" he queried his head tipped to the side.

Her hands came to rest on his chest, her twinkling eyes on him.

"We've never been normal, Alex," she said sobering and he went to speak before she put her finger over his lips. "We aren't normal, but I've come to realise in the last week that I love our *normal*. I wouldn't have it any other way. So yeah, you saying we were normal tickled me."

Alex nodded his head as he thought about what she said. "I guess normal is overrated anyway," he said and kissed her lightly.

Her body relaxed into him and he hissed as her pelvis rubbed against his stiff cock. "We should probably do something about that," she whispered against his lips.

"No time. We need to be at the airport in under ninety minutes." He groaned at having to deny themselves.

"We best be quick and save time showering together then." Evelyn slipped from his arms and sashayed towards the bathroom as he watched wondering how he had ever lived without her.

She stopped at the hallway door and turned, tilting her head to him, her eyes flirtatious. "You coming?"

Alex didn't need to be asked twice. They showered and he ate her pussy until she came, and she sucked his cock until he saw stars. Then he fucked her hard and fast against the shower wall. Once they were finished feasting on each other they packed and headed for the airport and the hell that was about to be unleashed on them and they did it hand in hand.

CHAPTER SEVENTEEN

STEPPING OFF THE PRIVATE PLANE EVELYN INHALED DEEPLY. There was something about the air in Monaco that just screamed indulgence. The place itself was one of luxury, decadence, indulgence, and sin.

With the highest rate of billionaires per capita than any other place in the world it also had the lowest unemployment rate in the world. The principality screamed wealth and not just new money. The Royal Family went back generations and were loved by the Monegasque people.

It was no wonder the building's, shops, restaurants, casinos, and harbour were so magnificent to look at. But with that came a price tag—real estate in Monaco was the highest in the world. It was because of those price tags, those casinos, and the temperate Mediterranean climate that it attracted a high-end clientele. People who wanted their every whim and wish catered to and that was where scum like Booth came in.

She felt a hand on her back and turned to smile up at Alex who looked pensive as he studied the area around the private landing strip. His eyes searching for any threat to them, his body shielding hers. He had been quiet on the short flight and she hadn't pushed it knowing that the traitor that was suspected in the Eidolon group was weighing heavily on him.

She too had been lost in her head, despite the threat Booth posed to them he wasn't the one that had her mind whirring. It was what would happen with her and Alex. Could they make it work or was their week of heaven in his Parisian flat all they could have? Would he see that she wasn't worth that hassle and having had his fill walk away from her? She didn't know and that doubt was not like her. She was always confident, always knew her own mind and went after it. But then nothing had ever mattered as much as Alex did.

"Siren!" Alex called and she knew from his tone it wasn't the first time he had said her name.

Instantly she bristled, she didn't want him calling her that, she wasn't that to him.

"What?" she answered sharply her head snapping up to meet his eyes.

"Gunner is here with our ride." A slight frown marred his sexy brow.

"Fine, let's go then." Evelyn headed towards the blonde god with the long hair, piercing blue eyes, and muscle for miles.

Gunner was hot if you liked that kind of thing. Personally, she liked her men taller with hazel eyes, golden blonde hair, and less bulk. The English man grinned when she reached him and opened the back door for her. She slid in and Alex climbed in beside her. Her body was stiff as she grabbed the seat belt and fastened it.

"*Mi nena*," Alex growled softly as he hauled her against him capturing her chin in his hand forcing her to look at him.

She tried to pull away twisting from him in the confined space. "What?" she asked again, and even she could hear the childish tone in her voice. She cringed inwardly that she could behave that way.

"You are *mi nena* and Evelyn in here," he said pointing to his head and then his heart and she felt the anger leave her at his words. "But out there, where the threat is real, you are Siren. You are strong and cold—a killer. They don't get to have that part of you that is soft and sweet and sexy. She is mine and I won't share her with people who wish her harm. So, stop pouting and kiss me."

His demand and the beauty of his words struck her so hard that she didn't hesitate or deny that was why she was pissed. She offered her mouth and kissed him as he lowered his head. When he pulled away the car was already moving but he didn't let her go and she was quite content to stay where she belonged—by his side.

They drove past Port Hercules and she watched all the superyachts in the harbour next to the school children having sailing lessons and marvelled at the diversity of the place. Small optimist boats next to moderate yachts, cruise liners, and then there were the oligarch's super yachts that were worth more than she would make in two lifetimes.

"What leads do we have?" Alex asked Gunner snapping her out of her reverie.

She saw Gunner glance in the rear-view mirror, noticing on further inspection the dark shadows around his eyes. Eyes that were giving nothing away as she watched him weigh his answer.

"We know which hotel he's in, but we don't know which boat or yacht the sale will be held on. We suspect it hasn't arrived yet," his slightly northern accent showing under the tiredness she could see.

"Makes sense. What hotel?" Alex asked as we drove away from the port towards a more residential area.

"The Golden Crowns."

"Shit. That will be swarming with security. We won't be able to get near him. We'll have to take him on the boat. We need to find out which fucking boat and get an invite."

Evelyn could feel his frustration. The Golden Crowns was the hotel where any billionaire worth his salt stayed and the hotel protected their elite crowd with an unmatched zeal.

The car stopped outside a gate that slid open as they idled. Gunner drove them through as Evelyn felt her stomach knot in a not altogether unfamiliar way. She glanced at Alex and saw he felt it too—something was off. Their safe house was meant to be small, residential, and unobtrusive. This hulking grand home with lavish turrets and well-kept shrubbery was not discreet.

"Why are we here and for that matter, where are we?"

Gunner stopped and turned to them. He didn't answer but he wasn't giving off any vibes that made her wary. "Plans have changed."

"On whose orders?"

Gunner didn't answer but opened the door and climbed out.

"What the fuck is going on?" Evelyn asked turning to Alex.

He shook his head as he swung the door open. "No idea but when I find out assess are gonna get kicked."

She had no doubt assess would fry, especially as Alex now had his 9mm in his hand. She followed him, watching as Gunner stepped through the door as a tall, gorgeous Greek god of a man stepped onto the doorstep with his hands in the pockets of his impeccably cut suit.

Jesus. If she weren't so busy mooning over Alex, she would be completely in a lust induced haze at the sight of the hunk in his custom designer suit that probably cost thousands and the watch on his left wrist that would keep her in cars for a good ten years. The two men stared at each other for a few seconds each sizing the other up. The tension almost palpable until Alex moved quickly forward.

"How the fuck are you, Hunter my man?" Alex asked as he

smiled and shook the outstretched hand, slapping the man on the back.

Evelyn let out a breath she hadn't known she was holding and felt the tension leave her. The two men pulled back and Evelyn felt the eyes of the Greek god—now known as Hunter—on her as Alex turned and held out his arm. She moved in close, her own arm going to Alex's back as his arm moved around her shoulder.

"Hunter, this is Evelyn Garcia. Evelyn, this is Hunter McKenzie. He's a very good friend to Eidolon.

"Miss Garcia, it is a pleasure to meet you." Hunter stepped forward offering his hand to Evelyn.

"Nice to meet you too," she responded noting his American accent.

"Please come in. I have offered Eidolon the use of my home here. I owe them a debt that I can never repay so I help when I can."

From his words, Evelyn knew there was an interesting story there.

"You don't owe us a damn thing." Alex was vehement in his response.

She followed as they moved through the reception hall which was all white marble floors and decorative balustrades leading up the double stairs to a mezzanine that went both left and right to more rooms. Distracted by the house and the new turn of events she gasped when a little boy no older than three came running around the corner. His dark hair and eyes were the image of Hunter. He was giggling but came to a sudden stop when he saw the new arrivals.

Hunter bent and lifted the boy into his arms as the child smiled. The boy looked at her before ducking his head into his father's neck and peering at her shyly.

"Say hello to Miss Garcia, Theo," Hunter said to the boy in a gentle tone that made her ovaries explode.

"Hello, Miss Gar.... Garc."

"Call me Evelyn."

"Hello, Miss Evelyn," he said shyly.

She grinned and turned to look at Alex who was regarding her with a soft look.

"Hey, Theo, it is very nice to meet you." Her heart turned to absolute mush over the adorable child.

Just then a stunning woman with long, dark, almost black hair with a blue streak in the front came running around the corner. She was beautiful—tall, slim, and striking with a pretty face and deep dark eyes. She also had a baby on her hip, this one a little girl with a pink denim jacket and pink animal print leggings. The woman was dressed in skinny black jeans, faux leopard skin ballet flats, and a cream shirt with a leopard print belt. She epitomised class but it was so understated and so approachable that Evelyn felt an almost instant liking for the woman.

"Alex." A radiant smile split her gorgeous face as she moved to Alex with her arm outstretched to hug him while holding the baby close.

"Good to see you, Lex. You're looking gorgeous as ever."

Evelyn felt a twinge of jealousy at his words before she pushed it down.

"You too, and who is the beautiful lady?"

"Lex, this is Evelyn Garcia. Evelyn, this is Lexi McKenzie." Alex pulled her tighter to his side. "And this adorable little one is Jasmine." Alex put his hand out so the baby could grab his finger which was immediately covered in baby drool, but it didn't seem to faze Alex. Evelyn saw Lexi look from Alex to her and back again.

"Oh my God, it's you. You're the one. The one he lost." Getting more excited by the second, Lexi pulled Evelyn in for a hug.

"Um—" Evelyn started, but Lexi kept right on talking.

"No don't say it. You don't have to. Believe me, I know true love when I see it and I can see it in you two."

"You'll have to excuse my wife, she gets rather excited about true love and wants everyone to be in love," Hunter said indulgently as he looked adoringly at his wife.

She moved to him and rested against his shoulder as he kissed her temple. "I just want everyone to be as happy as we are."

"I know you do, Blue."

There was so much love and tenderness in his voice that Evelyn suddenly felt as if they were intruding.

"Right, take the kids and get packed. We're going sailing for a few days so these guys can do what they do in peace." He grinned at Lexi's excited squeal.

She gave her and Alex a wave and ushered Theo away with Jasmine still on her hip.

Hunter turned to them, a serious look on his face. "I have no clue what the threat is but take all the time you need. My home is your home. Evelyn, I wish you well and hope to see you next time Alex comes to the US." With that he shook Alex's hand and then hers and was gone.

Evelyn turned and looked up at Alex her mind a whir from the last five minutes. "Well, that created more questions than it answered but I have a feeling that story had a happy ending."

Alex nodded as he looked in the direction they had just gone. "Yes, it did but it had a very hairy start and for a while it could have ended in absolute heartbreak. It's a story for another time though. We need to go see the guys and I need to kick Gunner's ass for the dramatics."

With that they moved towards the stairs and the sounds of laughter from Liam, Blake, Reid, and Gunner.

CHAPTER EIGHTEEN

They walked into the large office on the ground floor which now seemed to have morphed into Eidolon HQ Monaco style. The entire back wall had a sliding bi-fold door that led out onto a large patio with a heated outdoor pool with a vast decked area, BBQ, and even a pizza oven that would make most chef's jealous.

Alex looked around the spacious room with wooden shutters on the windows and realised that Lexi had been decorating. Finger painted pictures and children's drawings and scribbles were hung along one wall. He smiled to himself happy that everything had turned out for the couple.

"So, now we have a very luxurious safe house, but do we have any leads?" he asked dumping his bag on the cream couch and moving towards Liam and Gunner.

"Reid and Blake have gone to meet with a contact who says she might have something," Liam said with a smirk on his face.

Alex raised an eyebrow at that. As the blonde, cheeky, blue-eyed one of the group, Blake seemed to get more information from women than anyone else. He wasn't sure if it was his easy approachable nature, his cheesy charming flirty ways, or if he was just that good. But Blake could make a nun blush and then give away Vatican secrets. Perhaps it was his upper middle-class British accent or maybe it was because he seemed to genuinely like being around the fairer sex.

"Well let's hope he brought his A-game." He wanted this done and the threat neutralised so he could concentrate on finding out who the traitor was at Eidolon and convincing Evelyn to marry him.

"Does Blake even have a B-game?"

The grin on Gunner's face grew wider as Alex laughed. "Good point."

Alex caught sight of Evelyn stepping outside to make a call. She was pacing, her phone to her ear as she spoke, head down, her hair falling over her breast. She had been so sweet with Theo and his heart had beat so fast as he imagined her with their child one day.

Maybe if they had stayed together, gotten married, lived out their dreams as they had planned, they would have a couple of rug rats running around by now. Maybe even old enough to be in high school. He imagined a daughter that looked just like her giving him hell as she wrapped him around her little finger, or a son he could teach to play football or ride a bike.

"What you smiling about?" Liam had come up beside him.

"Nothing. Just thinking." He looked at his friend and hated the doubt that crept in wondering if it was him and dismissing it straight away. But then that was how he felt about all the team. No way would they betray Jack or Eidolon, it just wasn't in them. There had to be another explanation.

"Yeah. I guess having a woman like that look at you like she does would make any man think."

Alex twisted his head to look at him, hearing the slight wistfulness in his voice. "How does she look at me?" Alex was curious to know what others saw when they looked at them.

"Like you can solve climate change while cooking a three-course meal and saving the hungry of the world from starving," Liam replied as he watched Evelyn.

Alex turned back to her and at that moment she looked up and the smile she gave him was so natural, so sweet, and so sexy that his gut clenched as he fought the fear that flooded his body. If he lost her again, he was finished.

A world without Evelyn was cold, dead, lonely. He had existed for the last fifteen years but now he was living. He would rather be dead than live without her again. The morbid thought shocked him, but he didn't feel suicidal. It was merely a fact. He loved her so much that he honestly thought that if she were no longer his, his heart would just stop beating.

It had happened with his grandparents. His grandmother had died when he was a boy and not three weeks later his grandpa had died. His mother had always said he died of a broken heart. He had never quite understood it but now he did because he knew they would be that way.

"I would die for her," he said responding to Liam's words. He didn't take his eyes off her as she moved through the door and walked directly to him.

"I know you would, but we won't let that happen." Liam slapped him on the back and moved away to give them some privacy.

"What was that about?" Evelyn's eyes held a hint of wariness.

Alex pulled her close his hands going to her hips and hers flattened on his belly. "Nothing. Just finding out what Blake is up to. He's gone to meet a female contact. He has quite the way with women. Liam was worried his dick would drop off if he kept putting it where he shouldn't." He laughed as she pushed him and wrinkled her nose in distaste.

"Gross." She laughed.

He tossed his head back and laughed at her outrage. "Maybe but it is funny."

"Hmmm." She raised an eyebrow at him.

"Now, enough with talking about another man's dick. Let's go see if we can find where Simon Booth is and wipe the fucker off the face of the earth."

"I wasn't talking about his dick, you were."

"Woman, you're doing it now." His lips twitched at her indignation.

Evelyn was sexy as fuck when she was in a snit and he wasn't above winding her up a little to get her that way.

"Whatever."

She pulled away and moved towards Gunner, her sexy ass swaying as he watched. It was hard to concentrate when she was with him, but he knew he had to. It was time to get to work—there would be time to play later.

"What you working on, Gun?" he heard Evelyn ask as Lexi slipped in with a tray of sandwiches.

"I thought you might be hungry, so I sorted some food for you. There's plenty in the fridge and I left a pot of coffee brewing." She placed the tray which was loaded with chicken salad sandwiches and brie and cranberry wraps on the corner of the desk where Liam was working.

"Thank you, Lex. You didn't have to, but it is definitely appreciated." Alex smiled at the blue haired woman.

"It's no trouble and I know Hunt forgets to eat when he gets engrossed in work..." She let the sentence hang not needing to finish. She was right; he often forgot to eat when he was caught up in a case.

"Thank you, Lexi, for all of this."

"Alex, stop with that. If it weren't for you guys and Jack, I would probably be dead, and my son would be too. I can never repay what you did for us. So, let me make sandwiches and offer you our home. It's the least we can do."

He went to respond but she held up a hand, her finger over her lips. "No, enough." The finality in her voice made him chuckle.

"Fine. Thank you, Lex," he responded and then watched her leave the room. He felt Evelyn come up to him.

"She seems nice."

"They both are and neither deserved what happened to them." He offered her a sandwich which she took with a soft smile.

"Nobody ever does. It's always the innocents that get hurt."

He heard the pain in her words. "Mostly," he said as he cupped her neck, stroking her jaw with his thumb, "but sometimes love does conquer all."

Her head tilted as she looked at him from shuttered eyes. He knew the reason for the closed look. Evelyn was as terrified as he was that they wouldn't get forever, that this scumbag would rip them apart. He had no intention of letting that happen.

"Do you really believe that?"

"Yes, *mi nena,* I do because if I didn't, I couldn't do this job. But I know it will this time because I'll make sure of it. Nothing and nobody on this fucking earth is going to take you away from me." He saw her eyes flash with something he couldn't quite identify. "Do you believe me, Evelyn?" He needed to know she believed him.

She turned her head and kissed his wrist where he held her. "Yes, Alex. I believe you. I always believed in you."

"Good. Now eat up, we have work to do." He let her go and his phone rang before he could pick up his sandwich and he groaned but answered immediately seeing Will's number. "Alex."

"We got the time, date, and place."

As part owner—albeit a very hands-off owner—of Eidolon, Will provided the financial backing to do what they did. He was also the best hacker in the business. A fact that even their own

Lopez, who was ex-NSA and pretty fucking good on a computer, couldn't argue with. As Jack's brother everyone would have expected him to work exclusively for Eidolon, but he didn't. He worked for Fortis Security. He and Jack were only just getting their relationship back on track after a rift that had formed over a massive misunderstanding which he was not privy too.

Jack and Will were about as far apart as brothers could be both in looks and personalities. Both were tall and dark haired with blue eyes but that was where the similarities ended.

Jack was built like a brick shit house—muscular with a black and white attitude to loyalty and right and wrong. He was sharp with the best tactical mind he knew. He focused on the target and didn't stop until he'd accomplished his mission. A classic workaholic with a tendency to bury himself in his job.

Will by contrast was covered head to foot in tattoos and piercings and was less muscle-bound although he had bulked up of late. He had been a complete womaniser, rule breaker, and all-around bad boy until his girlfriend Aubrey had tamed him. Both were good men though and precisely who you wanted on your side in this situation.

"Tell me."

"Tomorrow night at eleven on board The Kratos."

"That doesn't give us much time." Alex could feel everyone's eyes on him.

"No, but if you can get on board, I have a way of keeping them busy while you find the file and deal with Booth."

"Which is?" Alex didn't want any surprises.

"Let me see if I can pull it off first," he said and then Alex had dead air.

He looked at Evelyn, Gunner, and Liam.

"Well, don't leave me in suspenders," Liam said impatiently while Alex tried to scrub his brain of that little image.

"Eleven tomorrow night on The Kratos."

"*Shit*. Do you know who owns that boat?"

From her tone he knew Evelyn knew who the owner was. "Yes." His jaw flexed as he tried to keep his worry out of his voice.

The Kratos was owned by the biggest heroin dealer in Europe. A man known only as Osiris, he was rarely seen and even when he was, nobody knew for sure it was him as it was believed he used decoys wherever he went. Named for the god of the underworld he was known to be brutal and regularly dispatched his own men for fear of them turning on him. He ruled by fear and was untouchable such was his power within the European Union. The funny thing was nobody could get a clear picture of the man. Sometimes he was shown as a balding overweight man, other times a young, suave handsome playboy.

"How the fuck we gonna swing this?" Alex could see the tension in Gunner's shoulders as the enormity of this job settled on them all like a shroud.

"I don't know yet, but we can, and we will. This fucker is not selling that document, and I don't care if I have to go through the entire European fucking army to get to him, I will."

"Sounds like I got here just in time."

CHAPTER NINETEEN

"PAX," EVELYN SCREAMED AS SHE MOVED TOWARDS HER friend and hugged her.

Pax hugged her back, the small smirk on her face as she leaned down to Evelyn. Pax was 5 feet 9 inches in her bare feet so in the skyscraper high heels she wore she easily reached 5' feet 11.

"How did you get in?" Alex asked as he moved behind Evelyn and wrapped his arms around her waist.

Pax surveyed him, her cool blue eyes assessing. "Well, you're every bit as delicious as I heard you were."

Evelyn smiled as Pax neatly ignored his question while Alex raised an eyebrow and Liam snorted a laugh.

Her eyes cut to Liam then, her sharp gaze moving over him until he squirmed before moving on to Gunner and she grinned. "Seems you only left the scraps for me," she said cuttingly, and Evelyn laughed at the pissed off looks that crossed Liam's and Gunner's faces.

"What are you doing here, Pax?" Evelyn linked arms with her and moved to the sofa. As always Pax was immaculate in a navy floral panel dress with three quarter length sleeves. The pencil skirt fitting tight around her curves before hitting just below the knee.

"Well, I got word there was a party on a yacht and you know how I love a party." Her flippant reply was pure Pax.

"You came to back me up." Evelyn felt warmth spread through her body and hit her in the chest knowing Zenobi always had her back.

"You didn't think we would leave your fate to Neanderthals, did you?" An exaggerated eye roll accompanied Pax's words.

"Hey, watch it. You might be a hot piece of totty with a cracking pair of Bristol's but saying we can't look after Evelyn is not gonna fly here. So, wind it in." Liam glared at Pax, his cockney roots showing in the face of the insult she had delivered.

Pax looked at her and confusion was plastered on her face before she let out a tinkling laugh. "What in God's name did he just say?"

"I think you offended him, so he was telling you that while giving you a compliment about your rack." Evelyn's face lit with a grin.

"Oh." Pax turned to Liam. "I apologise. I should not have implied you wouldn't protect Evelyn."

Liam nodded.

"Fine. Now that's sorted can you tell me how the fuck you got past security and walked in here?" Alex asked his hands on his hips.

"No." Pax's reply was succinct as she leaned forward to nab a wrap from the tray before standing and facing Alex. Evelyn shrugged at Alex who was now glaring at Pax.

"Bring me up to speed and I'll tell you how I managed to get us tickets to tomorrow night's auction though." She smirked at Alex

"On The Kratos?" Alex immediately felt his body tense.

"Of course," Pax replied with a head tilt that made her beautiful flaming red hair fall in a wave down her back as she did so.

"How the fuck did you manage that when we only just found out it was on The Kratos?" Alex folded his arms across his chest.

"Like I'm going to tell you that. Tell me, Alex, are you going to tell me how you managed to take out the warehouse full of meth dealers last year?" She straightened to her full height as she faced him, her good humour waning. "Because we both know that it had only been set up a few days prior and nobody should have known about its location. Yet you did. Care to share?" She waited silently as Alex glared at her, the silence stretching between them.

Evelyn fought the desire to get involved, they needed to work it out on their own. She wanted Alex and Zenobi in her life and had absolutely no intention of acting as the referee every time they butted heads. So much as she wanted to, she let it go although she was quietly pissed with both of them.

"Fine, Pax. Keep your secrets but I won't have Evelyn's safety put at risk."

"I guess we're on the same page then." Pax's smile was huge, and Evelyn could see how pleased she was at having bested Alex, or more importantly someone from Eidolon.

Evelyn looked at the door as Reid and Blake walked in, although walk was the wrong word for that pair. The prowled in like panthers looking for their next meal. Evelyn almost pitied the poor women they had been to see but not quite.

"We have the time, place, and Pax got us tickets. How many tickets?" Alex turned to Pax for an answer.

"Four and aliases to go with them. One for you and Evelyn and one for me and whichever hunk wants to escort me." She sent a smile in Blake's direction. Evelyn grinned as Alex rolled his eyes at Blake's grin.

"Let's get the details planned. We have a lot to do before tomorrow night."

Alex was in command again and Evelyn was surprised at how easily Pax seemed to defer to him.

Four hours later they had the details ironed out and Gunner had shown Pax to her room for the night. She was sitting on a large rattan L-shaped couch with white padded cushions in the fully enclosed patio with a glass of wine in her hand. The heat from the outside patio heater kept the chill from the air as she tucked her feet underneath her. Evelyn was totally relaxed and enjoying the relative quiet of the late afternoon where the only sounds were muted movements from inside the house and birds chirping in the sun.

Gunner and Blake had gone into the town to cruise the bars looking for any intel that would prove useful. Liam was in his room and Reid had slipped out saying he had a few things to do but wouldn't elaborate.

She felt Alex move behind her, the heat from his body warming her skin as he slipped his body behind hers and pulled her close. His arms around her gave her a feeling of safety and contentment as he pressed a kiss to her hair.

"You okay, *mi nena*? You've been quiet all afternoon."

"Yeah, I'm fine. Just a little anxious. What if something goes wrong?"

"Look at me, Evelyn." His tone was firm, and she slowly twisted her head to him. His face was fierce in the dusky light as he lifted his hand to cup her face. "Nothing will go wrong, *mi nena*. I won't let it. None of us will. We stick to the plan, get in, find the file, and get out."

"I know. I don't know why I'm worrying. I just have this pit in my gut that won't shut up."

"Is that normal for you?"

She knew from his tone he hated that he had to ask. "No, but then I don't normally do this with the man I love," she replied putting her heart out there on the line for him to take or crush. Evelyn held her breath while she waited for him to speak.

"I won't let you down, Evelyn. Just keep a cool head and we'll be back home in no time at all and can plan what happens next." His arms tightened around her and she felt tears prick her eyes at the way he had ignored her declaration. "I'll tell you one thing though, when we get home, I'm going to tie you to the bed and never let you leave. I love you too much to even contemplate life without you. So, you can relax those muscles and stop fearing the worst. I would never treat such a precious gift as your heart with anything but respect and gentleness."

Her body relaxed and she lifted a hand to stroke his jaw. "I love you so much, Alex" She followed her declaration with a soft kiss. He let her take the lead not pushing to take over but allowing her to explore until the kiss became heated as their need burned bright and white hot.

"I love you too, Evelyn. Don't ever doubt that you are the other half of me. You've held my heart in your palm since you were six."

"Yeah, I kinda stole it." She laughed feeling lighter and more confident.

"No, *mi nena,* I gave it to you freely," he murmured as he stood and grasped her ass in his hands, lifting her until her legs wrapped around his waist.

Evelyn grinned a lopsided smile and pressed her body into his. "I haven't finished my wine." She nuzzled her face into his neck inhaling his scent as it sent a jolt to her pussy. She had always loved the smell of him.

"Fuck the wine, I want to taste that sweet pussy." He held her tightly as he stalked inside past a grinning Pax and up the stairs to the room they were sharing. His words sent heat pooling in her belly as her pussy throbbed with the need for him.

Her Alex had acquired a dirty mouth since they were younger, and she fucking loved it.

"Tell me more," she said as he pushed open the bedroom door with his shoulder before slamming it with his foot and turning to pin her against the door, her legs still around his waist, his hard cock pressing against her sensitive clit.

"I intend too." His smirk was the last thing she saw before his mouth crashed down on hers.

CHAPTER TWENTY

ALEX HAD SENT LIAM WITH PAX TO PICK UP SOME DRESSES for her and Evelyn to wear. Liam had grumbled but obeyed the order following the redhead as she sashayed out to the car as if Liam was her chauffeur. They had made it back within two hours and he had helped carry the outfits and an assortment of other things upstairs and to Pax's room where she and Evelyn were getting ready.

He watched as Reid walked into the office that had been turned into a war room decked in black fatigues. A knife was strapped to his thigh, one in a holster on his shoulder, and Alex knew he had one in his boot.

"We all set?" Reid's voice was voice calm, his southern accent barely there. Reid was always calm in a situation which was why he was running point on this from the outside. As an ex-member of the FBI hostage rescue team he was cool under pressure and a fantastic shot. He and Blake were like chocolate dipped churros as far as the other sex was concerned.

Being from North Carolina, Reid had that sleepy drawl going on that women couldn't get enough of. Add to that his impeccable manners, his ma'am this and ma'am that, it was a sure thing that boy would get his rocks off. Unlike Blake who was the resident slut, Reid kept his conquests close to his chest.

"Nearly. Just waiting for the others and then we'll go over the plan one last time before we roll out."

Reid was leaning against the door jamb his posture relaxed as he folded his arms over his chest. He lifted his chin in assent not bothering with words when none were necessary. Alex felt the uncomfortable niggle in his gut—could Reid be the traitor? He didn't think so as it didn't fit his personality. Alex let the thought go. He couldn't think about that now he just had to do his job and pray he could trust his men. As soon as he got back to Hereford though he and Jack were going to figure this shit out.

Gunner and Liam moved in next also wearing black fatigues. Liam was needed for the explosives on the boat and Gunner had secured them a small aircraft in case they needed to get away quickly. Blake was posing as Pax's date for the night which enabled him to use his close protection skills to monitor the room around him while staying close to Pax and Evelyn.

"We're just waiting for the ladies and Blake," Alex said as he watched Liam move to the couch and settle in.

"You hear from Ambrose's fiancée at all these days?" Gunner directed his question to Liam.

Alex saw Liam stiffen just a tiny bit before he relaxed. He didn't think anybody else saw it, but he had, and it made him wonder. It could be completely innocent as Liam and Ambrose had been like brothers, growing up in the same area as kids. Losing Ambrose to a head wound which caused a brain bleed had been a blow to them all, but most especially Liam.

He had gone to work for Fortis for a while after not coping with the death of his best friend and needing to be close to home to help Ambrose's fiancée deal with losing the man she loved while having a young child to raise.

Eidolon had missed him and after a few months he had come back but he wasn't quite the joker he had been before his friend's death. He was still the best explosives expert on the team, or any team for that matter, and still a solid operator, but he had a slightly wilder streak now. Almost as if he was playing with fire and didn't care if he got burned.

"Na, haven't been up to see her for a few months, been busy."

Alex immediately knew Liam was lying. Why lie about it? It made no sense to him. His thoughts were stopped from further speculation when Pax walked in the room followed by Evelyn.

Alex felt every hair on his body respond to the vision in front of him. Dressed in a dark burgundy gown that was covered in tiny sequins and beads, it was slashed to the thigh and dipped low at the front to flash her amazing cleavage. Spaghetti straps held the moulded cups which barely covered her magnificent tits. A band of flesh coloured see-through net fit under her breasts showing off an inch of skin all the way around from the edge of her armpit across her ribs and upper abdomen to the other armpit. Alex went totally silent as she walked to him on champagne coloured stiletto satin sandals with tiny ankle straps. Dangling crystal earrings containing a tiny tracker hung from her ears.

"Do I pass muster?" Her soft laugh made his dick twitch. Her arms outstretched she gave him a slow spin to show the extremely low back on the dress before facing him again. Her dark, sultry hair was down and curled over one shoulder the end sitting over her left breast.

He pulled her to him so that her body was flush to his from hip to toe. The fingers of his right hand skimming the soft skin of her back as he kept the other in the front pocket of his tux, fearing if he put both hands on her they would not be leaving this house for many hours to come and that could not happen.

"You are so fucking beautiful that I can hardly think straight," he said barely growling the words into her ear lobe before his teeth bit down on the soft flesh. He felt her shiver in his arms and fought the grin.

"You're pretty handsome yourself in that tux, Mr Martinez." She looked up at him and touched her tongue to her bottom lip to moisten it. He loved that he could do that to her but the way she affected him was fucking criminal.

"You going to call me Mr Martinez when I fuck you while you're wearing those sandals and nothing else later?" He didn't care that the others were listening in to their conversation while they waited.

"Oh, most definitely." Her words ended on a purr, and he chuckled at the sexy eager sound.

"Well, let's get this show on the road so I can get to the part of the evening where I get to fuck you." He turned her around, patted her ass, and moved away. Again, he didn't trust himself having her close while his libido was going nuts. "Right, let's go over the plan one last time. I don't want any fuck ups. Do you all understand?"

"Yes, boss," they all choroused although Pax and Evelyn said it with a smirk.

"Evelyn and I will arrive first using a taxi-boat that Gunner will be driving. Fifteen minutes later, Pax and Blake will arrive. Liam, you will be in the boat with us hidden from sight. You will then exit the boat and slip onto the bottom deck as it's docked with The Kratos. The proximity to the boat will give you some cover from the guards patrolling the top decks but you'll only have a short window while we distract them for you to get on the bottom deck. You'll then set the charges in case we need them later."

Alex turned to Reid. "Reid, you'll follow in the same way with Pax and Blake." He turned to Pax. "You'll need to make sure the distraction is enough to make the guards look the other way."

Pax tipped her head. Her hair was in a fancy updo that he had no idea how to describe. The long black gown with white lace detail at the top fitted her like a glove and he could see why men got distracted by her. She was stunningly beautiful but did nothing for him. Hopefully the guards wouldn't feel the same way.

"You just worry about you and I'll do my job." The eye roll that accompanied her words seemed to be her go-to communication.

"Fine. Evelyn, you and I will look for the file. Pax and Blake, you stay close to Simon. If he moves, I want to know. After the charges are set Liam and Reid will take out the guards below deck. We'll sweep Simon's private quarters. It must be somewhere on board. My best guess is he'll have it on him, that's what I would do. If we have no luck, Pax, you lure him back to his room and we'll take him there and get what we need from him. We know some of the players but not all of them, so be on your guard. Our covers are in place and as far as we know nobody knows us or should recognise us. Evelyn, did you ever meet Petra in person?"

"Yes, but I was using a disguise. She didn't know what I looked like. She thought I was a blonde, and I went by Siren," with her."

"Good, so we should be good." Alex looked around the room. "Any questions?"

"What happens if shit goes south? I don't feel happy blowing the boat with so many people on board."

Evelyn's question caused anger to rise inside him, the threat against her and the risk she was taking weighed heavy on him. "Those people are skin traders, drug dealers, pimps, arms dealers, and killers. I have no qualms about us blowing the boat."

Her face softened as she laid her hand on his belly and his muscles tightened at her touch. "Yeah, I get that but what about their dates and the servers on the boat?"

Alex felt his anger ebb when faced with her softer side and he gently stroked her cheek. "Evelyn, I can't risk you for some faceless innocent."

"I know but I can't live with myself if innocents die to keep me safe."

Alex knew she wasn't being awkward, she genuinely cared about people, especially those she considered innocents. "Fine. Liam, fix the charges so they don't blow the boat but incapacitate it. But not until we have Simon in our custody. That should give everyone time to get to safety."

"Sure thing, Shadow," Liam said using Alex's code name.

Evelyn was obviously Siren, Reid was Captain Kirk as usual, Gunner was Viking, Blake was King because he had protected so many royals, and Liam was Pyro for apparent reasons. Pax was Gucci because she only wore designer or so Evelyn had told him.

"Right let's go. Remember if we get separated, we meet back here. If nobody else arrives within an hour, contact Jack or Roz and ask for an extraction. Stay safe and let's get the job done." He took Evelyn by the hand and was about to walk to the hallway to help her with her coat when he was stopped by Pax.

"Alex, do you have a second?"

Alex made sure she could see his irritation at the interruption on his face as he let go of Evelyn's hand, nodded, and headed towards the library.

Alex waited for the door to close behind them before he spoke again. "What can I do for you, Pax?"

"How much do you know about what happened to Evelyn?"

He felt his spine stiffen. "She told me everything." He could feel bile crawl up his throat as he thought about what she had been through.

"Did she tell you about David?"

"Yes, he was her handler and he died of bone cancer." Dread filled him and he wondered why Pax was bringing him up.

"No, he didn't." He could hear caution in her voice as if she was debating if she should say anymore or not.

"I'm guessing you called me in here for a reason and it wasn't so we could shoot the shit with half answers and statements. So, why don't we skip this verbal dance and get to that part?" He was barely holding on to his temper, frustrated at the game Pax seemed to be playing.

Pax smiled her intelligent eyes showing him there was a sharpness in her that he could respect. "You really love her, don't you?"

"Okay we're done." If she wasn't going to tell him what she'd intended to, he wasn't wasting any more time. He certainly had no intention of discussing his relationship with Evelyn with her.

"No, wait."

Alex stopped at the door and turned around.

"David's real name was Arthur Roach. He was married to Belita Fuentes." She let that hang as Alex took in the name and quickly connected the dots.

"Omar Fuentes daughter?" She nodded. "Start talking and make it fast, Pax."

"Arthur worked for Omar, but he was not a bad man. What Evelyn said about his wife and daughter dying in a skiing accident is true. But he never worked for the cops, he was a trafficker. Because he had connections with the police and government, he managed to work his way in and pose as Evelyn's handler. Once he got her away, he hid her in Courchevel."

"But why?" Alex was confused as to why he would do it and go to so much trouble to protect Evelyn.

"Here." Pax passed him a picture. The woman in it was the image of Evelyn.

He looked up sharply. "Who is this?"

"His daughter Estrella Fuentes. The one who was killed. By all accounts, Arthur had been trying to get them out of Fuentes' control when they were killed."

"So, he saved Evelyn because she looked like his daughter but why fake his death?"

"Arthur got hungry for power and he knew that if he sent

Evelyn to Roz, she would train her and eventually Evelyn would go after the men that killed little Ellie and thus the men who had also killed his own daughter and free him to start his own operation. He always blamed Fuentes for the accident whether it was true or not I don't know?"

"How do you know this?"

"Because Arthur is Osiris!" Pax held his eyes as she dropped the bombshell.

Alex felt a haze of red fall over his eyes as he tried to get a handle on his fury. His hands clenched and he felt a ringing in his ears. "And you're only sharing this now?" He barely managed to suppress his desire to wring her neck.

"Because I wasn't sure until fifteen minutes ago. I had hoped he wouldn't be there tonight, but our intel tells me he will be. Although that could change any minute."

"*Fuck.*" He spun on his heel and paced as he tried to figure out if they should abort the mission.

"So, you've known who Osiris was all along and didn't tell us?"

"Zenobi doesn't owe you anything."

"No, but last I looked Evelyn was Zenobi and she deserves more than all of you lying to her." He knew the verbal blow had struck when Pax winced, but he didn't care.

"You're right. We do owe her more, but you have to understand. Evelyn loved David or Arthur or whatever the fuck he calls himself, and it would break her heart to know he betrayed and used her."

"And what the fuck do you think it will do when she finds out you, Roz, and everyone else did?"

"We wanted to protect her."

"Yeah well, good fucking job." He snarled as a knock sounded, interrupting them.

"Come on, Shadow, time to go." Liam poked his head in and

looked between them with a question in his eyes that Alex ignored.

"Yeah, give me two minutes."

"Sure." Liam closed the door behind him.

"So now what?"

Alex advanced towards her as she held her ground. He bent closer and, in a voice so filled with ice it was a wonder the room didn't freeze, spoke, "Now we go and pray like fuck that Evelyn doesn't spot him because if she does and something happens to her nothing on earth will stop me from finding you. When I do, you will all pay for betraying her." He forced himself to turn and walk out while he still could.

As he moved towards Evelyn, she looked at him. He could see the worry in her eyes which he hated, so he plastered a fake smile on his face and kissed her to distract them both. The kiss was hard and filled with passion and anger and she took it, instantly making him feel better as he poured his fear into the kiss before pulling away.

"Everything okay?" Her eyes went to Pax who had walked out behind him.

He turned and looked at Pax hating her for dragging him into this and making him lie to Evelyn. "Yes, just a minor detail Pax wanted to share."

"About?" He could see suspicion peek through the question.

"I'll tell you later. It's nothing important."

She regarded him for a minute and then nodded. "Let's go then." Evelyn took his hand in hers and led the way to the cars.

CHAPTER TWENTY-ONE

THE SMALL TAXI-BOAT BOBBED UNDERNEATH HER AS EVELYN huddled into her faux fur wrap next to Alex. Her gaze slid to him, his profile strong and handsome. He seemed alert but relaxed to anyone watching. Like the sexy arms dealer his cover insisted he was. Only someone who knew him well would be able to see the tension in his shoulders, the tight-lipped smiles.

He was hiding something, and it had to do with Pax. She would bet her last penny on it but what could she possibly have said to make him so angry? As her hair swept back from the breeze of the ocean she shivered and reached up a hand to smooth it back in to place. Alex caught her hand in his and brought it to his lips. The boat started to slow but she was mesmerised by the look in Alex's eyes.

The emotions she saw there frightened her and made her beat faster. "What is it, Alex?" she asked gripping his thigh.

"Promise me that whatever you see, you'll do as I say even if it seems odd to you?"

Something horrid slithered into her belly at his words. "You're scaring me, Alex."

"Please, *mi nena,* promise me."

She felt the desperation in his words. "Okay. I promise but I need to know why."

"I can't tell you right now but let's say some things may have come to light and all is not what it seems."

"You're asking too much."

"I know and I'll explain everything as soon as I can but for now, I need you to trust me. Can you do that?"

Evelyn thought about what he was saying and over the last few weeks—God since the day they had met. He had never given her a reason not to trust him all he had ever done was love her. "Yes, Alex. Of course."

"Good girl." He kissed her softly as the boat began to slow as they neared The Kratos. "Showtime." he said as the boat stopped, and he stood, offering her his hand as one of the guards leaned down to help her up.

He was tall and very muscular with the pale skin of someone who spent all his time in the gym rather than exercising outside. His face had acne scars which he had tried to cover by growing a full beard. Dark brown hair cut short but styled with some sort of gel, the suit he wore was black and off the rack but not a cheap one. His dark eyes as they swept over her body were assessing but not overtly sexual. She took his hand and stepped up ready to put on the performance of her life so Liam could slip onto the lower deck unseen.

Deliberately turning her heel, she made as if she was going over on her ankle grabbing for the guard with a shriek as if to catch herself. The man looked panicked as he grabbed her arms to steady her as she fell into him and pushed him backwards.

"For God's sake. Diana, you're such an idiot." Alex spat taking up his role in the charade. "I can't take you anywhere without you bloody embarrassing me." He grabbed her arm from the guard and shook her slightly.

Evelyn glanced a look at the guard and saw his jaw flex at the way Alex was speaking to her. She had read him correctly. "I know. I'm sorry, Henry. I should be more careful." She lowered her eyes as she said the words, her voice meek.

"Yes, you should, or you might find the next accident is more permanent. I can't have you making me look like a fool all the time."

Evelyn lowered her eyes again in submission, tearing slightly as she looked at the guard who was vibrating with anger. His eyes were trained on Alex and Evelyn glanced down and saw Liam was gone and their job was done.

She slipped her hand into Alex's, their signal that all was well.

He looked at her, his face softening before he brought her hand to his lips and kissed her knuckles. "Why do you test me so when you know how much I love you?"

She smiled as he pulled her into his body, and they moved away. Evelyn stopped and turned to the guard who was still watching them as Gunner steered the taxi-boat back towards the shore. "Thank you," she said politely her eyes downcast once more as a smile played on her lips.

She saw him blush a little at her attention before nodding. "You are very welcome, Miss," he said before turning away and resuming his watch of the approaching boats.

With her arm tucked into Alex's they moved towards the main deck where the party was already in full swing. Waiters in white tuxedos were walking about with trays of Champagne and canapes. Alex took two glasses from a passing waiter and handed her one with a tilt of his head in the direction of the port side. Evelyn took a sip from her glass barely letting the alcohol past her lips. As she looked up her eyes swept the deck and she caught sight of Simon Booth.

He looked dashing in a Tom Ford Tuxedo, the obligatory blonde bombshell clinging to his arm. She barely looked legal and had to be no more than nineteen or twenty. He was holding court with a group of four men and three women.

She felt Alex lean in and despite the fact they were working, her body responded to his closeness. His lips touched her ear so that to the outside world he looked affectionate. Her body shivered at the contact giving even more credence to their cover. Not that it was an act in any way, he just had that effect on her. "The two older men are brothers and outwardly industrialists, but they also sell arms to the highest bidder. The woman is—"

"Helena Romavich. She's an ex-model who now has her own stable of girls for the highest paying clientele," she finished for him.

He pulled back and smiled down at her before lightly dropping a kiss on her lips, his face showing his pride in her. It shouldn't make her feel so happy that Alex was proud of her, but it did.

"Let's mingle."

They moved through the crowd waiting to catch sight of Pax and Blake. Her gaze drifted across the sea of perhaps a hundred people. Either famous, disgustingly wealthy, or criminals, and in some case all three. She saw the leader for the opposition party in the UK, a renowned food critic who thought it was prime television to rip peoples dreams to shreds live on air, and a Hollywood movie star who had just signed with the biggest television studio in the business as a leading man for a new rom-com series. On his arm was the famous model Calista Lund.

Evelyn was a little disappointed to see her here, they had met once at a charity event she was attending for Zenobi and she had seemed sweet. If she was dating that guy she was in for a shock because he had more boyfriends than she'd had hot dinners.

In her mind she tried to pick out the major players, the ones here for the actual auction rather than the party. She counted probably ten who were significant contenders. There must be hundreds of weapons on board this yacht. They were swimming with some dangerous sharks tonight—she just hoped she wasn't the one that ended up bleeding.

She and Alex had positioned themselves beside the railing on the main deck with their backs to the sea, limiting the chance of any surprises, when they spotted Pax and Blake.

Alex nudged her arm as he turned and looked out to sea before speaking into the comm. "Everyone in position?"

Evelyn laughed to cover the movement of his lips in case anyone was watching. Making it seem as if he had said something to make her laugh. A chorus of checks lingered over the headsets as they prepared for phase two of the plan.

"Keep your eyes peeled for Osiris. I want to know the first second anyone gets an inkling he's on board."

Evelyn heard something odd in his tone as he issued the instructions. A weighted feeling of doom settled in her as her neck hairs bristled making her shiver. *Someone's watching me.* She turned to look for the culprit in the crowd and found nothing suspicious but movement from the sun deck caught her eye and she saw a silhouette of a man move away from her view.

Evelyn shook off the feeling and focused on the job at hand. She would tell Alex as soon as she got a second. Remaining vigilant she swept her eyes over the sun deck again looking for a ghost and finding nothing except a pair of lovers engaging in a stolen kiss. Her body relaxed as she let the feeling of dread go laughing inwardly at her own paranoia. That was what being hunted did, it made a person see things where there was nothing to see.

Blake and Pax moved towards them, Blake waving his hand and drawing mild attention as if they were old acquaintances.

"Henry, it's good to see you." His voice sounded like he'd had the royal plumb well and truly shoved up his ass and was just a tad louder than socially acceptable.

"Carter, good to see you." Alex held out his hand for Blake to shake.

"Have you met my wife Vivian?" Blake introduced Pax and Alex.

Alex took her hand and shook it briefly as he then made the introductions to Evelyn. She could see they had caught the interest of Simon who was slithering his way towards them. Blake's cover as Carter Mountford was the draw they wanted to lure Simon.

Carter Mountford was a real person—he had been a diamond thief and playboy. What he wasn't was alive having been killed during a raid by Eidolon but due to his resemblance to Blake, they had kept his death a secret so they could use the cover. Will had dropped the odd speculative news item onto the web making people think he was in fact alive and going about his scoundrel's life. Zenobi had done similar things so she hadn't been shocked when Alex explained it to her.

"Carter Mountford?" Simon asked taking the bait.

Blake turned, a look of bored arrogance on his face. "Yes. Who wants to know?"

"Simon Booth. This is my party."

Evelyn could hear the excitement in his voice as he held out his hand as Blake shook it.

She and Alex politely disengaged with nary a glance from Booth who was regaling a very bored looking Blake with a story about Eton. As per the plan she would slip off to the toilet and then try and get into Booth's private quarters while Alex stood guard.

Squeezing his hand, she raised up and kissed his cheek. "I need the little girl's room."

"I'll wait here. Let me hold your drink." His role of attentive boyfriend was well and truly in place.

Making her way down the narrow, dark walnut wood walkway towards the stateroom she passed the galley where she could see kitchen staff busily milling around waiting for the chefs to give the order for the trays to leave. She saw maybe eight wait staff and two chefs with probably another ten up on deck making twenty staff so far.

Glancing around quickly she saw a guard move towards her from further up the corridor. He wasn't like the guard from earlier. This one was tall still but less bulky and was genuinely handsome with brown hair and hazel eyes. He was almost boy-next-door pretty if it wasn't for the massive scar that ran from his right brow-bone and across his cheekbone ending at his chin. It gave him a terrifying look which matched the frown he was wearing.

"You can't be down here, miss," he said sternly but without suspicion, his lilting accent making her think he had spent a good amount of time in Ireland.

"Sorry. I was looking for the ladies' room. Can you help me?" she asked softly making sure her voice was non-threatening, flirtatious even. She knew the others could only hear her when she activated the two-way comm on her bracelet but to do so now would make it dangerous.

"Yes, of course. This way." He held his hand in front of him for her to proceed him as he led her back the way she had come.

She needed to get past him and into that stateroom. He led her down a different direction from where Alex was standing towards a large saloon and as he walked her through the room Evelyn started to get a gnawing feeling in her gut. Something was off. He was leading her towards the sun deck and that wasn't right at all.

Suddenly the feeling of doom from before, the prickle on her skin came back as he pushed her towards some steps. She faltered and turned coming face to face with 9mm Glock. Her eyes moved up and she saw the dead look of someone who didn't care that she was a woman or that she was weak. He was doing a job and that was the only thing he bothered about.

"Boss wants to see you," he said his voice almost lyrical.

Evelyn shot him a glare but said nothing as she climbed the steps to meet the boss.

CHAPTER TWENTY-TWO

WHEN EVELYN'S FOOT LANDED ON THE TOP STEP, SHE SAW A man with his back to her standing looking out to sea, one hand in his pocket the other holding a cigar. She didn't know what it was, whether it was the familiar way he stood or the woodsy sweet scent of the cigar, but her belly filled with poison as the impossible started to take root.

A hand in the middle of her back pushed her forward so that she almost tripped onto the large sun deck complete with small jacuzzi. The motion made the man turn and as their eyes connected, the twisting brutal pain of betrayal lanced through her.

"David?" she asked with a shake of her head as if she couldn't quite believe what her eyes were telling her.

"Evelyn, my dear girl. You look so well. Love suits you." He moved forward taking her hands in both of his and holding them out so he could look at her in the fatherly way he always had.

"I don't understand. I thought you died. You had cancer. I nursed you. I watched you until you became too sick to see me." Evelyn could hear the remembered pain in her voice she'd felt at losing the only person who cared about her.

"Come sit down, Evelyn. You look like you're about to faint." David took her hand and led her towards a sun lounger and pushed her to sit.

Evelyn took a moment to breathe, composing herself while she ran the facts in her head. But they refused to come to any other conclusion than the one she didn't want to make.

David had aged but he looked well, his hair grey but styled, the paunch he'd had before he got sick now gone. The clothes he wore were of designer variety and the watch on his wrist was a real Rolex not a cheap knock off. Add the fact the guard had called him the boss and she kept coming to the same conclusion.

"David, what is going on?" she asked as she studied him. He had cared for her, looked after her, trained her until he could no longer and then he had sent her to Roz.

"My name is Arthur Roach. I'm afraid I lied to you, my sweet girl. You see, I was not a handler for the American government. I worked for Omar Fuentes." She could see the sadness on his face as he spoke, and she couldn't hide the gasp of surprise or the pain his words evoked.

"What?" she asked as she felt the blow as his words hit and took it, pushing it down deep so she could deal with it in private later.

"Let me start at the beginning. I was born in Chicago to parents who worked to keep the wolf from the door until it killed them. They worked hard, paid taxes, and were good people and it got them nothing but an early grave. I wanted better so I worked for a local gang running drugs, working my way up until I caught the attention of one of the higher-ups. I was young, fit, eager to do anything to get me out of the hell hole I called home."

Arthur began to pace as he spoke outlining his rise until he moved to Miami. "I started to work inside the inner circle and then one day I met her, the love of my life. Belita Fuentes. She was

Omar's youngest daughter. Sweet, kind, beautiful, and she loved me, but Omar would only sanction the marriage if I started working his other business for him. He wanted someone inside the family to run the trafficking side and I was the man for the job. At first, I was flattered. We married and were so happy when little Estrella was born. She was the light of my life. I started to see what I did was wrong. The guilt ate away at me every time I looked into her cherubic face. I needed to get my family out, but I was trapped."

Evelyn had never noticed it before, but David—Arthur—was selfish. He had been happy to take the money until it no longer suited him. He'd had choices and those choices led to that. "I guess he didn't want to you to leave?" she said instead not sure who the man in front of her was and not wanting to rile him.

"No, he did not." He shook his head sadly.

"What happened?" Tucking her hands underneath her legs she went to activate the comms mic.

"I took them to Courchevel on holiday. We spent the whole time planning how we would make our escape. We were so close and then the accident happened, and they were taken from me." He sat down beside her and with a sad look grabbed for her wrist pulling it from under her and shaking his head. "Why, Evelyn? Why betray me. I was not going to hurt you. I just wanted to clear the air so we could keep things friendly between us." He ripped the bracelet from her wrist as he spoke, dropped it on the deck, and smashed it under his foot.

Evelyn glared mutinously at him. "So why all this?" She gestured with her hands to encompass the yacht.

"Simon is a young boy who thinks he's a big fish. He needed an ally and I needed a distraction. When I faked my death and set you on the path to kill the rest of the Fuentes cartel to free me, I thought life would be different. Now I am richer than God himself and yet I still find myself unfulfilled."

"So, you knew I would go back and kill them?" The feeling of being used did not sit well with her.

"Evelyn, of course. You had so much rage, so much untapped potential. I gave you the tools to free us both. I made you what you are today."

"And the child I found? Ellie. Did you kill her too?"

"That was unfortunate." He pushed himself to his feet angrily and walked away from her.

"Unfortunate? She was a baby. You killed her and you call it unfortunate? What kind of fucking monster are you?" she asked finally letting her temper get the better of her.

"I am the man who saved you."

She could hear his fury in every word as he spoke to her and responded in kind. "You are the monster who nearly destroyed me. The police never knew about me, did they? I was just a runaway kid as far as they were concerned. You faked the attack on me to isolate me, to make me run and trust only you. That was why you let me keep my name and wear the necklace. You knew nobody would be looking for me, not really. I would be just another missing teenager." As she said the last words the full impact of it all hit her and she hugged her arms to her belly.

"No, Evelyn, they never did."

"So how did you come to be outside the police station that night?" she asked wanting all the details to make sense.

"I was in a car further down making sure those goons didn't fuck up. I saw you run and knew where you would go. I drove there and intercepted you, it wasn't difficult."

"Everything was a lie and I trusted you,"

"But don't you see. We could be great you and I. You are the daughter I lost. I miss you." He said the words with feeling, and she believed him.

"But I have a father, one I've not seen for over fifteen years because of you." She blinked, trying to force away tears of grief and anger. "You manipulated me from the very beginning. My parents and Alex were never in danger, I could have gone home."

"I will change your mind once we have renewed our friendship, you will see."

She needed to find out about the hit on her. "What about the price on my head?"

"I will keep you safe, Evelyn."

"So, you weren't the one that set me up?"

"No, that was Simon. He was annoyed with you for taking his lover away from him," he said with a wave of his hand as if it wasn't relevant.

"I need the file, Arthur."

"I will get it for you if you come with me."

She saw for the first time the cold ruthless businessman he was and had always been. "I can't." She prayed that he had some affection for her still and would honour her wish.

He moved towards her and raised his hand, as she struggled to stand still. Cupping her cheek, he looked at her sadly. "If you change your mind then let me know. I will be watching."

Evelyn let the grief at what she had lost wash over her as she watched him walk away from her.

"Be happy, Evelyn, and tell your Alex to take care of you or I will gut him."

She had no doubt that the man in front of her would do just that. She knew she should stop him, he was a criminal, he was Osiris, but she couldn't make her feet move. She could see some of the man who had dried her tears and cared for her in him. She wasn't foolish enough not to see the Stockholm shit she had going on. She ran to the edge of the deck as he disappeared and watched as he boarded a small speed boat. He turned once to look at her and lifted his hand to wave just as a bullet lodged in his body making him fall to his knees. Shock was evident on his face as an explosion rocked The Kratos.

CHAPTER TWENTY-THREE

ALEX WAITED AND WAITED, HIS BRAIN WAS SCREAMING AT him that something was wrong, and Evelyn shouldn't be taking this long. Why hadn't she activated her mic? He had tried to contact her with no luck and the knot in his gut was screaming to him that he needed to move. After fifteen minutes he knew he couldn't wait any longer and activated the comm on his watch so the others could hear him. "Shadow has lost contact with Siren. Be ready to execute stage three." He kept his voice low knowing the sensitive equipment would pick it up.

"Pyro in place," came Liam's reply.

"We have the Joker in sight." Blake replied using the code name they had given Simon Booth.

Moving in the direction Evelyn had gone he passed through the busy kitchen. Seeing nothing amiss he walked to the stateroom she had been headed for and using the lock pick from his belt was inside in under ten seconds. Slipping through the door he saw nothing out of the ordinary—no sign of a struggle, nothing knocked over but also no Evelyn. Deciding to do a quick search to make sure he hadn't missed anything he moved through to the small but very lavish bathroom and stopped dead. The guard from earlier, the one who'd helped Evelyn on board was slouched on the floor, his body crumpled, blood splattered behind him from a single bullet to the head.

Alex cursed and activated the comm "This is Shadow. We have a body in the main stateroom. A guard from the boarding platform."

"Roger that. Moving towards your position," Reid answered.

Alex wasted no time, moving out of the room after checking the hallway and clicking the door closed. The desire to find Evelyn was burning in his blood now and his steps quickened. *I've got to get to her. I can't lose her again.* The mantra repeated over and over in his head.

His body jolted as an explosion rocked through the boat. He threw his hand out to catch himself as he was thrown forward. Steadying himself he began to run as he heard screams and shouts from outside.

"Pyro, what the fuck?"

"Wasn't me, Shadow." Alex could hear Liam running as he spoke.

"King, Gucci, do you have eyes on the Joker?"

"Negative." The reply made him shudder.

"Find him. Captain Kirk, meet me on the sun deck. Viking, get in position for exfil."

"We have a speedboat leaving the yacht," Viking said over the comm.

That could be Simon Booth.

"Confirm?" His foot hit the bottom step of the deck.

"Fuck, we have a second boat leaving. People are abandoning ship like rats. I have eyes on Siren," Gunner said a second later. "She just jumped in the water and is swimming towards one of the boats that's now idling.

"Fuck, fuck, fuck." His feet hit the deck and he scanned it for Evelyn. "Where did she jump from?"

"Sun deck, starboard side."

Alex ran to the starboard side and looked into the inky black sea trying to make out Evelyn. He caught sight of her as she pulled herself into a speedboat. His relief was short lived though as another explosion hit and the boat began to lilt dangerously.

"We need to get off the yacht. I have eyes on Siren. Do you have the Joker?"

"Negative."

"Prepare for exfil." Alex turned and froze. Simon Booth was in front of him, holding a gun in the hand that was outstretched and pointed at his chest.

"Well, it was a nice try, Alex."

Alex raised his hands in a gesture of submission as he assessed Simon. His hand was steady on the gun, his clothes barely wrinkled. In fact, he looked calm and composed, nothing like a playboy with a god complex who had an evil streak a mile wide should look.

"Nothing to say?"

Alex glared at him not willing to take the bait.

"Maybe this will help you get some perspective." Booth pointed towards the boat Evelyn was on.

She was standing in the boat with a man beside her who had a gun to her head. Alex fought the desire sweeping through him to tear Simon to shreds with his bare hands. He even took a step before checking himself when Simon lifted the gun aiming it at his head.

"Tut, tut, Alex. Your training should be better than that."

How in the fuck does he know my real name and that I'm trained?

The poisonous worm in his belly twisted as the obvious conclusion came to him. The traitor was on this mission with them. He railed against it, but the evidence was there. He had no time to think about it now, he had to get to Evelyn.

"What do you want?" he asked through gritted teeth as the boat listed to the left.

Out on the night sea boats were swarming as people fled, some even jumping into the water in fear. His eyes barely left Evelyn who was standing statue still. He wondered why she wasn't fighting back. She was highly trained, he knew she could probably take out that one man, but she wasn't even attempting too. Something was wrong.

"What I want is for us to take a little trip. You're going to call your men off and we're going to leave on that boat." He motioned to Gunner who was already in their boat.

"He's never going to let that happen," Alex sneered thinking perhaps he had been correct about Booth all along.

"He will because if he doesn't, I will kill Miss Garcia and then have my sniper take him out before I take control of the boat."

Alex saw in his eyes he would do it. The man wasn't insane though—just fucking evil.

Alex was going to enjoy killing him. "Fine let's get this shit over with." Alex started to move towards the steps feeling Simon behind him.

"This is Shadow. I need everybody to stand down. The Joker," he said and took great joy in hearing the angry hiss of breath from Booth when he realised it was him, "has Evelyn and will kill her if anyone makes a move. Follow protocol." Protocol was to head back to base and get fucking planning. "Viking, we're headed your way."

Alex moved down the steps his hands out in front so as not to freak Booth.

"Through the galley," he said pushing him in the back with the barrel of the gun.

"I'm gonna shove that gun so far up your ass if you don't stop pushing me." Alex's tone was almost conversational.

"I don't think you're in a position to give me orders."

Alex agreed but he would be and then the fun would begin but not for Booth. Oh no, his days on this earth were over. The second he'd made Evelyn a target he'd signed his own death warrant.

They approached the main deck and were met by two guards who cuffed him with cable ties before grabbing an arm and manhandling him towards the boat as Gunner watched. His face was a mask of calm, but Alex could almost feel the barely checked fury in him. Not a lot of people knew but Gunner had some serious anger issues when he was younger. He had learned to control them years ago but if the way his jaw was working was any indication then he could blow and allow the rage to be set free. Alex made eye contact trying to communicate with him to calm the fuck down. He didn't need to deal with him while worrying about Evelyn.

They got him on the boat and secured him by tying his ankles together, leaving one guard to hold a weapon on Gunner. The ship dipped as Booth stepped on board and nodded to the guard. Alex had a gut-clenching second where he knew what was going to happen but could do absolutely nothing about it as the guard pulled the trigger and red bloomed. Shock crossed Gunner's face before he fell backwards into the water.

"Let's go."

Alex lay still trying to not to let sadness overtake him as he worked on a plan to get away and help Evelyn. But until he knew where they were going all he could do was wait and watch and conserve his energy. The image of Evelyn wet and bedraggled, still looking stunningly beautiful as she stood silent and still on the boat, came to him. He tried to figure out what was wrong with the image, he couldn't help thinking she blamed him for something.

CHAPTER TWENTY-FOUR

Less than a minute after Evelyn, saw Alex being pushed into the small speedboat a needle had been jammed into her neck and everything had gone black as she felt her body turn to lead and her legs give way. She'd felt arms around her, probably that Irish asshole who held the gun on her, then nothing until now.

The cold was the first thing she noticed. A shiver racked her body and the biting bone-deep cold seeped through her consciousness. The heavy, damp fabric of her dress clung to her skin. Her feet were bare, and she could only just touch the freezing concrete floor with her toes.

She was hanging by her arms, the height of the hook such that she felt as if her shoulders were going to pop out of their sockets any minute. The ache in her back, neck, and arms made her want to cry in pain but she wouldn't. She would never show weakness to an enemy—it wasn't her style.

Her brain tried to remember what had happened. She had watched the bullet hit Arthur and jumped into the water. Not because she wanted to save him but because the sight had knocked her out of the shocked state she was in and she'd realised she couldn't let him get away.

He had been kind to her but only for his own gain. He had taken more from her than he had ever given and then she'd thought of how he had reacted to little Ellie's murder like it was a broken fingernail or an inconvenience and not the life of a precious child. All his talk about wanting to get out had been bull-shit he'd fed himself, so he didn't feel like the piece of shit he was.

When she had pulled herself on board, however, that Irish asshole had been there and held the gun on her threatening to set off the second explosion on the yacht if she moved, so she had remained still, barely breathing. At that time Arthur had been breathing but unconscious.

Now she was here in this freezing cold and windowless room, the cinderblock walls giving her no clue to where *here* was exactly. A single light hung from the middle, but the light was weak, and she couldn't make out much from her place in the corner. There was a dark metal door on the left opposite corner to where she was hanging and nothing else except a single wooden chair which was too far away to be of any use and a camera that was blinking at her.

She needed to figure out where she was and who was holding her. She had seen Simon Booth as he'd walked Alex away and her belly clenched painfully as she thought of Alex. He was alive, of that she had no doubt. To even entertain anything else was unthinkable and so painful she couldn't go there.

With a wash of guilt, she realised what she had unwittingly put him through by not getting in contact for all those years. Now she knew why David had kept on about the danger to her family if she ever went home. So much so that even when the threat was over her fear still stopped her. What if the job she now did for Roz put them all in danger? She had known who and what Alex was, but she had to admit to herself at least that her fear of rejection from him had stopped her. If she ever got out of this hellhole, she would try and make it up to him somehow. Evelyn knew he had forgiven her—such was Alex's big heart. But she needed to make amends with her family too and stop the pain she now acknowledged she had caused by staying away.

The door to the dungeon, for want of a better word, opened and a flood of light filled the space as Irish walked in. Evelyn stayed silent as he moved closer, stopping just out of reach.

"I brought you some dry clothes." He laid a pair of tracksuit bottoms and a long-sleeved thermal vest beside her feet. She continued to glare at him in silence and he quirked a brow at her. "Nothing to say?" he asked with a sneer.

"What do you want? My eternal gratitude for kidnapping me, asshole?" she hissed.

He chuckled and crossed his arms over his chest waiting. She hated that he was good looking. All assholes should be ugly fucks, especially the likes of him.

"You finished?" She stared at him silently. "I'm going to let you down but if you try anything, I'll knock you out again. And believe me when I say I'm one of the nicer men in this place. You do not want to be unconscious when some of the others see your pretty little ass."

The warning was clear and while she might be furious, she wasn't stupid. She needed all her wits about her in this shithole. "Fine."

He moved closer and lifted her off the meat hook she was suspended from. Evelyn tried not to cry out as blood rushed back into her shoulders. The pain was almost unbearable, but she kept silent. *Never show a weakness for them to exploit.* Roz's words rang through her mind. He cut her ties and stood back; his arms folded again as he waited.

Evelyn looked at the clothes then at him. "Charming." She knew her tone was waspish, and all she got was a dead look for her trouble. This guy was in charge. She hadn't figured out who he worked for yet, but he was most definitely at the top of the tree. It was on the tip of her tongue to ask him, but she knew he would never answer her outright, so she let it go.

Turning her back to him she reached down and pulled the damp cold material from her body and let it land in a wet heap on the floor. Squatting so as not to flash him her ass any more than she had too she quickly pulled the bottoms up her legs and slid the thermal over her body. The feeling of warmth was instant, and she was grateful for that small mercy. If there was one thing she hated, it was being cold.

"Thank you."

He moved closer, tied her hands, and placed them over the back of the chair he had pulled into the middle of the room and secured her tightly every move made in silence. She didn't fight him figuring that she would bide her time until she had an escape planned and knew precisely what she was facing. She wouldn't get past him in this six-foot square locked space anyway.

He picked up the wet dress and walked to the door before turning back to her. "Don't thank me. If you don't cooperate, you'll wish I had let you die of pneumonia by the end of the day."

He left and she heard the lock clang into place. Evelyn watched the door and thought on his words. Who did he work for? Simon? She had thought it was Arthur, but he had left her with no malice and a promise of help if she ever needed it. That didn't fit either.

Her mind went around and around until she almost drove herself mad. She felt her eyes drooping but forced them to remain open, not wanting to get caught out by any of the pigs Irish had talked about. But the next thing she knew her head was shooting up at the sound of the door opening again. Instantly alert she watched as a more muted light filled the space denoting late afternoon. That meant she had been here about twelve hours by her guess.

The doorway filled and anger seared through her as Arthur walked in. He wasn't showing any signs of being shot, yet she had seen it with her own eyes. Evelyn knew it was easy to fake a gunshot, but she hadn't thought that was the case. He moved closer, Irish standing behind him, and she fought not to show her emotions as her heart beat faster and her blood rushed through her body. The desire to do this man harm intense.

"Evelyn." His greeting was soft before he came to stand in front of her close enough that she could see the knife he held in his hand. It was a hunting knife and wickedly sharp looking.

"David. Nice to see you recovered from getting shot," Evelyn could hear the ice almost dripping from the word as she watched the knife from the corner of her eye.

"You should have come with me, Evelyn. There would have been no need for all this," he twirled the knife in the air close to her face, "unpleasantness." His smile didn't reach his eyes. He ignored her comment about getting shot though.

"So, all that 'I'll be watching', acting like you cared about me was bullshit," she hissed.

"Not at all. I have always kept a close eye on you. I do care about you which is why I tried to do this the nice way. Your stubbornness has forced my hand and I need your cooperation."

"Oh, of course, let me just bend over backwards to help the child murdering scumbag." Her tone was derisive, and she knew she had hit a direct blow when he stiffened.

The blow was swift, sudden, and caught her by complete surprise, and her head was thrown back from the force of it. Pain exploded in her right cheek, blood filled her mouth, and tears sprang to her eyes from the pain. Lifting her head, she blinked the tears away and smiled at him. "Now we see the truth," she said through a mouthful of blood.

"Don't make me do that again," he said in a strangely calm tone she didn't recognise.

This was the man that got the name Osiris. The dangerous drug lord, human trafficker, and killer. "There is something I need, and you're going to help me get it."

"How am I going to do that?" She was curious despite herself.

"Simon is nothing more than a front man. He stole the file because I told him to but setting you up was his idea. I allowed it because it played into my plans perfectly. I knew if they thought you were guilty, the British Monarchy would send the hit to their favourite little hit men," he said with a dismissive wave of his hand. "Eidolon coming after you made you run, and you did exactly what I hoped. You ran to our place." The way he spoke and the tone he used made her feel dirty.

"And how did it help you?" she asked keeping a close eye on the knife he was waving.

"Someone paid me a great deal of money to bring Eidolon and its team members out into the open. Someone who wants them all dead." A smile of satisfaction crossed his face.

"That is fucked up." She shook her head in denial.

"Yes, it is but, none the less, it is fact."

"So, let me see if I have this straight. You had Simon steal the file for you in the hopes that it would expose Eidolon. Simon then had me set up for it which still helped you because you knew the hit would go to Eidolon. But Simon has double-crossed you and now you need me to get the file and expose Eidolon to save my ass and yours. Is that right?"

"Insolence is not pretty on you, Evelyn." She saw Irish take a tiny step forward.

"So why do you need the file in the first place or is that just a perk?"

"The file is worth millions of pounds to the right people." He shrugged.

So, it was money and power—the age-old desire for men like him.

"What is on the file?" She wanted to know why she was strung up like a plucked chicken.

"According to Simon the file proves that the current heir to the throne is adopted and is not rightfully fit to rule."

"Wow, and he knows about this how?"

"I have no idea, nor do I want to. I'm a businessman and the how's and why's do not matter. Now, I need your word you will cooperate."

"Again, what is it exactly that I'm supposed to do?"

"I need you to bring Eidolon out into the open." His voice was filled with triumph.

She wanted to laugh at the thought that she would betray Alex and therefore Eidolon. "No."

"You will, Evelyn, or I will make you wish you were dead." He flipped the knife before stepping back and allowing Irish to step forward. Evelyn knew this would hurt but nothing—no money or threat—would convince her to expose or betray the man she loved and the team she now considered friends.

"Do your worst, Osiris." Evelyn looked him dead in the eye, her voice cold.

Irish stepped up and landed the first blow to her stomach stealing her breath and making her gasp. She didn't cry out or show her pain. The next two blows landed on her ribs but each one on a different spot. The blows rained down until she felt delirious with pain, but she still didn't cry or scream.

When they stopped, Irish stepped back, and she let her head fall forward as pain began to radiate through her.

"I will leave you to consider my proposition. We will be back first thing in the morning to see if you are more amenable." Arthur stroked her hair in a gentle, fatherly way that almost made her sob. He then nodded at Irish who left with him.

Evelyn let the tears come then, hidden by the darkness,

allowing herself a very brief respite before she pulled herself together and thought on all she had learned.

One thing kept puzzling her. Who knew enough about Eidolon to want to expose them and which of them was a traitor? She knew Arthur didn't know or he would have told her. He wasn't shy about telling her information which also meant he had no plans to free her or let her live. Could she fake it and agree to help him and then get back to Alex? *No.* Arthur was far too clever for that and he would have a plan in place.

Her only hope was to stay alive long enough for Alex to come get her and he would. She had no doubt in her mind about that. When he did, Osiris would know what real pain felt like. Until then she would take whatever they dished out and pray she was strong enough to take it. Her mind went to Roz. She knew her story and what she had gone through and she had been barely a child. If she could survive so would Evelyn. Unfortunately, sometimes you weren't the one that had to endure.

CHAPTER TWENTY-FIVE

ALEX HAD NO IDEA WHAT SORT OF OPERATION SIMON HAD going on, but it became clear to him very quickly that the men he was using were not as highly trained as the ones on the yacht had been. The house they had taken him to was not far from where they were staying with Hunter. They hadn't covered his head either so he could see the way in, the number of guards on the gate, and weak spots in their security.

It meant they were probably going to kill him at some point, but it also meant they had no idea who they were dealing with. They had removed his comm unit but left him dressed and the watch with the tracker was still transmitting, meaning his team were not far away. Even if they weren't, he could probably free himself in a few hours.

They had pushed him into a bedroom with nothing but a divan bed with a single sheet and a blind on the window. They had at least taken his guns and knives from him. The ties at his wrists were still on but would take less than a few seconds to cut through. They probably thought that he had no weapons available to him, so he wasn't much of a threat—one man against all of them. They didn't see the bigger picture. The bed sheet could be used as a noose or to choke someone out and that was completely ignoring the fact that his whole body was a finely honed weapon.

Being taken was possibly a good thing. He now had a chance to find the file and get the fuck out of there so he could find Evelyn. Walking to the window he saw the glass was double glazed and the window nailed shut. Outside the night was quiet, the smoke from the fire lingered on the air with the sea breeze blowing inland.

He felt nausea fill him at the thought of Evelyn out there with some maniac. His bet was Osiris. He fought the desire to punch the wall in anger. If Pax had warned him earlier, he would have taken more precautions, but she had sprung it on him, leaving him nowhere to go. If he had warned Evelyn she could have reacted badly and thrown the mission to hell and cancelling the mission wasn't an option.

They'd had one window to get the file and clear her name. Now it was fucked, and she was missing. His only saving grace was that perhaps Osiris had some affection for her and wouldn't hurt her. But if he knew Evelyn at all—and he did—she would lose her shit when she realised she'd been manipulated and all the connotations that went with that. Like losing her family, her friends, her future with him.

Yeah, it was fucked. She was in trouble and he needed to get out of there and go find her before she ended up in a world of hurt.

The door opened behind him and he looked around feigning boredom as Simon walked inside flanked by two guards. Both men seemed muscular but unfit. They probably relied on their size and not any skill. Typical muscle for hire scenario that almost made him laugh out loud. Simon had removed his jacket and was in his tux shirt and trousers. He was unarmed which was also interesting. Maybe he didn't have the stomach for it.

"Mr Martinez," Simon said making it clear that he knew his full name.

"Mr Booth." Alex smirked at the obvious power play.

"I am not sure what you find so amusing but I'm sure this will wipe the smile off your face." He produced an image of Evelyn in her wet dress strung up by her arms in a cinderblock room. Her head had fallen forward and provided evidence of her unconscious state. He swallowed past the lump of fury in his throat and sought the cold, calculated coldness that he would need to think straight and get her free. Looking at the image again he saw her clothes while wet, were not ripped and she had no apparent injuries. He also knew that the night was young.

"No response, Mr Martinez? I would have thought seeing the woman you love hurt would provoke some kind of reaction," he said with a sneer.

Alex couldn't wait to wipe the floor with his fucking stupid face. "She's strong. She will be fine until I can get to her." His calm answer hid the worry he felt, but he knew it would be convincing enough to trick Simon.

"Wow, you really are a hard bastard."

"So, what do you want me for?

"Someone wants you dead and they're paying me a pretty penny to make it happen. More than I would have got for tonight's auction if you hadn't fucked that up with your bombs."

"That wasn't me." He shrugged ignoring the titbit about someone wanting him dead. That wasn't news, some fucker always wanted to kill him.

Simon angled his head as if he was assessing what Alex was saying for truth.

"Hmmm, interesting. If it wasn't me and it wasn't you, then who was it?" Alex asked filling the man with doubt. "Maybe you have a snake in your midst?" Alex gave a chuckle and hoped his words would fill the man with doubt.

Simon went red, his face angry and mottled before he released his breath and un-balled his fists. "The only one with a traitor in the camp is you."

So, Booth knows about that too. There seemed to be more going on here than he'd first thought.

"Who added the second team to Evelyn and blew up her house?" He didn't really expect an answer but asked anyway.

Simon it turned out liked the sound of his own voice. "Whoever is paying me to kill you. I have no name. I just take the money and do the deed."

"So not Osiris? I know you're his little errand boy now," he said using some guesswork.

"Osiris thinks he can beat me by using Evelyn, but he can't. Whoever it is that wants you and the rest of your little friends dead, is serious. He's pitting some of the meanest, deadliest criminals in the world against each other to bring you down. Whoever delivers gets the money and the kudos. I want both."

"So, he pits you against Osiris? That's a step up for you." Alex kept him talking hoping to gather as much information as he could.

"Osiris is old, he needs to be put out to grass. The business needs new blood and I'm going to take it from him."

"You are a real piece of work, aren't you? No wonder your cousin disowned you." He made sure his voice was filled with all the contempt he was feeling.

"My cousin will rue the day he challenged me," Simon snarled. "Now, enough with the chit-chat I have to go and deliver this file to its new owner and collect my payment." He reached inside his trouser pocket before waving a data stick at him. "Then I can come back, deliver your dead body and collect my payment."

"Yeah, have fun with that." Alex kept his tone bored as he watched Simon and his goons leave. That had been a very enlightening little chat and he knew he needed to find Evelyn and finish this once and for all. "Oh, one more thing," Alex said as the three men turned to leave.

Simon turned back impatiently his hand in his pockets—the fool. "Yes?"

"I'm going to need that stick."

He moved so fast Simon never saw it coming. Snapping the ties that the idiot guards hadn't made sure were secure, he spun, grabbed the gun from the waistband of the closest guard, and looped his forearms around Simon's neck in a choke hold while holding the gun on him.

Alex backed towards the door as he kept a close eye on the guards who both had their hands up. He had seen another man downstairs and two on the gate. Not great odds, but he'd certainly faced worse.

"You and I are going to take a little walk," he said to Simon who was breathing hard before focusing on the first guard. "You, take the sheet off that bed."

Obeying him the guard walked to the bed and ripped the sheet off.

"Now, strip. Both of you." The men blanched at the order. "Now." He made sure they saw him removing the safety on the gun. Both guards began to strip until they were standing in their boxers.

"All of it." The men glared at him but pushed their boxers off. "Now kneel and wrap your arms around each other."

"No fucking way." The smaller guard made a move towards Alex.

Alex fired a round into his foot and the man screamed. He now had less time and the remaining guard downstairs had probably been alerted.

"Do it or the next one goes in your dick." He looked the man in the eye, so he knew he meant every word. No man would risk his junk getting shot off no matter how big of a badass they were, and these two were far from that. He watched the men get down in the position he had instructed. Keeping the gun to Simon's head he focused on him next. "Tie them together and use their shirts to gag them." He chanced a quick look out the door for the third guard as Simon tied the men together.

"You won't get away with this." Simon's voice held much less conviction than it had before.

"Yeah, yeah. Whatever you say. Now throw me the data stick." He held his hand out. Simon removed the stick and tossed it to Alex. "Let's go." He turned to leave almost barrelling into Liam's smiling face.

"Mate," he said with a smile as his eyes landed on the red-faced guards, "that's just cruel." He laughed loudly and shook his head.

"Where's the other guard?" Alex asked trying not to let his suspicions get to him.

"Reid took care of him. Blake and Pax took care of the guards on the gate."

"Gunner?"

"Took a round to the shoulder but he can still drive one-handed."

Alex felt relief course through him. "Let's go. I have the file." He shoved Simon at Liam who soon had him cuffed and knocked out with a brutal uppercut to the chin. Bending, Liam threw him over his shoulder and Alex followed down the stairs but not before closing the bedroom door and snapping the handle off. He had no beef with the guards, they were doing a job—a shitty one, true—but he saw no reason to kill them.

They jogged down the long drive as the sun was rising on the horizon. The deep dark blue of the night giving way to the bright yellow and orange of a new day. When they reached the front gate

Blake, Gunner, and Reid were waiting with Pax who stood a little behind Blake.

She looked stricken and he felt a moment of sympathy for her. She loved Evelyn and considered her family much like he did his teammates. She wouldn't have done this intentionally. He couldn't offer her anything though, he was barely holding it together himself.

He climbed in beside Gunner who was wearing a sling and sour face, clapping him on his good shoulder. "Through and through?"

"Yeah. Be good as new in a few days."

He knew Gunner was downplaying the pain of getting shot. No matter what the movies said, getting shot hurt like a mother fucker and he knew Gunner was in pain but was still determined to help.

"I want a sitrep on Siren right now," he demanded turning to Blake once Simon was secured and everyone was in the vehicle. Alex used her code name to maintain his distance and whisper-thin control.

"The signal on the tracker you gave her is out. We have Decker running the satellites to see if we can get some images and Will is running the cameras on all the ports from Marseille to Genoa. We *will* find her, Alex."

Alex swallowed his fear of not knowing where she was and fought the guilt he felt. He had promised he would keep her safe and here she was, again missing at the hands of a fucking sociopath.

"We'll talk when we get back to base. I want to know exactly how this fucking happened." He smashed his fist on the dashboard causing the others in the car to look at him in shock. He didn't act that way, throwing punches and breaking things. Jack—yes. Alex was the cooler of the two, the more relaxed second. While he did have a temper, he never got physical, but this was different. He looked at Simon who was the cause of everything that had happened. "I want him stripped and put in a shed out the back."

"Sure thing, boss." Liam cast a glance at Reid after he spoke. Alex knew they were concerned for him. He was holding it together—barely and he was acting a little out of character. He let the look go though.

Reid had been quiet so far, not saying anything which wasn't unusual for him though. The rest of the short journey was made in silence, everyone pissed off at the disaster the mission had been and the resulting chaos.

When they got back to Hunter's home, Simon was hooded, stripped, and thrown into an old empty metal shed that should have housed garden equipment but thanks to Reid was now empty. He would have to ensure the house and grounds were put back exactly as they had found them when they left.

Taking the stairs two at a time, Alex went straight to the room he had planned to share with Evelyn for the duration. The scent of her perfume hit him as soon as he walked in and he tried to smother it as he walked to the bed and sat down heavily. Exhaustion was like a heavy cloak on his shoulders. He dropped his head in his hands and took a minute to allow the fear to wash over him. He had operated most of his life not knowing where she was, but this, this was so much worse. Knowing she was probably hurt, beaten, or God forbid worse, made him want to puke.

The feeling of helplessness almost paralysed him. He needed to take everything he was feeling, find an outlet, and purge it. He knew just the person that could help him with that.

Standing he forwent the shower he was going to have and instead stripped off his tux and put on combat pants and a black long-sleeved tee-shirt. Slipping his feet into military style boots, he ran down the stairs and into the office.

Reid, Liam, and Gunner were standing by the desk and Blake

and Pax seemed to be having a heated debate in the corner when he walked in.

He stood looking at them for a second. "I want to know what the fuck happened last night." His voice was a growl. The men looked at one another and then Pax began to speak. Alex thrust a finger at her. "Not you. Anything you had to say was null and void the minute I found out you betrayed her." He could see the violence in his voice directed towards a woman, shocked the men around him.

Blake stepped towards Alex, anger in his usually jovial eyes. "Hey, come on."

Pax put a hand out to stop him. "No, Blake, he's right. We did lie to her, but we never did it to hurt her. We love her."

"Well, you have a funny fucking way of showing it," Alex hissed as he watched his teammate bristle with violence towards him.

"Maybe, but I want to help right that wrong and you need me."

"No, Pax. I don't fucking need you." He moved towards her slowly. He could see Blake watching him like a hawk, seeming ready to step in if Alex showed any sign of aggression. "But Evelyn does so you can stay." He looked at Blake. "And you decide whose fucking team you're on and quick." Alex then turned to Liam, Reid, and Gunner. "Now, give me everything we have before I go spend some time with Booth."

He heard the door slam behind him as Blake stormed out with Pax following close behind. "I guess I have my answer." His tone was soft and deadly.

The others stayed silent not used to this unseen side of him. They updated him on what they had which was fuck all and then he had Liam put in a call to Jack to update him.

He couldn't speak to him right then. He was barely holding his shit together and Jack would be on the next flight out dragging his ass home if he thought for one second Alex had lost focus.

"Reid, you're with me. Gunner, I want everything we have on Osiris," he clipped before walking out the back door and heading to the metal shed.

He would get what he needed out of Simon or the man would die a slow painful death.

CHAPTER TWENTY-SIX

ALEX SLAMMED HIS FIST INTO THE BLOODY PULP THAT WAS Simon's face one more time before he let the man's head fall. He had no time to start slow and build this shit up, he needed information now. The man had a broken nose two black eyes and his lip was split and Alex had only just started. "Tell. Me. Where. She. Is" he growled his voice almost feral.

"I told you, I don't know."

"Wrong answer." Alex reared back and hit Simon's ribs this time. Four more blows and he asked again. "Tell. Me."

"I don't know where she is." Simon's head lolled forward as the pain made him weak.

"You know, I can do this all day, but I don't have the time and neither does Evelyn. I'm just going to start shooting off bits of you that I don't need starting with your feet before moving to your knees. Then that useless little dick of yours goes. But first, I'm going to let Reid break both your arms." He stepped back and nodded at Reid.

Reid stepped forward and tossed the cigarette he had been

smoking on the ground before standing in front of Booth and blowing smoke in his face. Reid then calmly grabbed Booth's left arm that was tied behind his back to the chair and hooking his forearm through, bent the elbow joint and snapped his arm with barely any pressure.

The scream that tore from the man was loud and piercing and made Alex glad that the house was secluded.

"And the other one," Alex demanded.

"No," Simon screeched snot and tears running down his face as Alex crossed his arms and stepped forward giving a chin lift to Reid to tell him to stop.

"You know what I want."

"He'll kill me if I tell you."

"I'll kill you if you don't. I'll make sure it's painful," Alex countered and nodded at Reid to do the other arm.

"No. No." Simon screamed and started trying to scoot back on the chair with his bound legs.

"He has a small house on an island not far from here. He would probably take her there."

Alex could hear the defeat in Simon's voice. "How many guards?"

"I'm not sure. Twenty maybe."

"I want the exact location."

"It's called Capraia. You can't miss it. It's the only mansion on the island."

"The Islanders are loyal?" Alex wanted to know if they would be facing them as well.

"Some." Simon's voice was slurred, and Alex could see he was starting to drift into unconsciousness. Alex went to leave with Reid behind him. "Wait. What will you do with me now?"

"Nothing." Alex turned, lifted his gun, and fired putting a bullet between Simon Booth's eyes.

The man's body slumped forward, shock the last expression on his face before it went slack in death.

Alex turned to look at Reid expecting judgement but there was none on his face.

Reid shrugged. "He would have been a constant threat to Evelyn. A man like him holds a grudge."

Alex and Reid had started to cross the lawn when Blake walked towards them. "Did you get what we need?" Blake gestured to the shed with his chin.

"Yes, I hope so. Osiris has a place on an island called Capraia."

Alex glanced at Reid as he lit another cigarette.

"You with us?" Alex saw the pain on Blake's face the question garnered.

"Can't believe you would ever doubt me after what we've been through together," Blake replied his jaw hard.

"No, but I can't believe you sided with Zenobi."

"Come on, man. I didn't side with them. I'm with you one hundred percent, but Pax is an ally and we don't treat women like that. We do a lot of shady shit, but we never go after women—ever. You were crossing a line."

"You finished?" Alex knew some of what Blake said was true, he had crossed a line.

"Yeah, man, I said my piece."

"Fine. Get your shit and tell Pax to get hers, we're going to Capraia." He started towards the house before stopping and turning to Blake who was grinning. "And for God's sake, fuck her already and get her out your system before Evelyn gets back and breaks your balls for fucking her friend over."

"Fuck off, man. It ain't like that."

"Oh, it's definitely like that." Alex could see Reid's smirk as he stubbed his cigarette on the wall and binned it.

"Anyway, when I tell Evelyn what you did," Blake shouted at Alex, "it ain't my balls you're gonna need to worry about."

Gunner looked up as the three walked in. "Get what you need?"

"Capraia. Pull up the maps." He leaned over Gunner's shoulder who was typing one-handed.

"Move out of the way." Liam took over, typing at a much quicker pace. The maps showed an island that was surrounded by dark patches of rock indicating getting a boat close would be a fucking nightmare.

"Shit." Gunner leaned back and surveyed the map.

"We need to bring in the rest of the team. An assault like this needs more frogs in the sea and men on the ground," Gunner said.

"No. If we do that we risk being seen by the villagers. We don't know if they are hostiles too." Plus, after what Booth had told him about wanting the team exposed that would be the perfect way to do it get them all together and then *boom*. "We need another way."

"I could put a call into Roz. She could have someone here in twenty-four hours!"

"No. Not to be an asshole, Pax, but I don't know your girls that well and I don't trust them. Not because of what you all did but because I don't trust anyone I haven't worked with. It isn't personal." He held up his hand to stop Pax and noted that Blake kept his trap shut about the subject.

"Fair point." She nodded her head in understanding.

"What about the ferry?" Liam pointed to the screen. "We can go in with the tourist group."

"And a group of men and one woman won't look suspicious as hell?"

"We could tell them we're shooting a porno." Liam winked which made Pax glare and give him the finger.

"How about Fortis?" asked Gunner. "We can see if Lucy and Roz are available and they might even be able to send a few of the guys as back up."

"That could work. Let me put in a call to Jack and see what he thinks." Alex moved towards the patio door. If he was going to get his ass handed to him by his boss, he didn't need everyone to hear it. Hitting call, he waited for Jack to answer.

"Go." Jack had answered the call in his usual brisk fashion.

Alex could tell by his tone he was pissed. "Are we secure?" He heard Jack moving around on his end.

"Yes."

"Osiris has Evelyn on an island called Capraia. It's a ferry ride from Livorno which is six hours drive from here."

"I'll send Decker, Waggs, Mitch, and I'll come—"

"No, we can't do that." Alex was quick to interrupt Jack. "Booth said that the same man is paying both him and Osiris to draw us out and expose us. Whoever it is, wants us all dead."

"Fuck." The word had a wealth of meaning but right then it showed how pissed Jack was. "You can't do this on your own. She'll be heavily guarded if Osiris has her."

"I know, and Pax suggested Zenobi, but I don't trust them enough. We have no clue who the fucking traitor is or who they are working with or for but best guess—the fucker wants us all dead."

"Agreed."

"I want Fortis. We can get onto the island by ferry, but a bunch of men is going to be a major red flag and we have no clue about the fucking locals. If we can get Lucy and Roz and maybe a few of the guys, then we can go in with a few couples and it will look less conspicuous."

"Let me talk to Zack. His kid is due any day now but if he can spare them, I know he'll help."

"Fine. Call me back as soon as." Alex went to disconnect.

"Alex?"

"Yes?"

"What are we doing about Simon Booth?"

"He's been dealt with."

"Dead?" Jack asked but he already knew.

"Yep. Couldn't take the risk he would come for Evelyn again."

"Good. I'll get a clean-up crew to the house just as soon as I call Zack. Then I'll see if he can send Daniel. You might need a medic as Wagg's can't go."

The thought was like a giant pit opening in his gut. The idea of Evelyn hurt in any way was like a physical pain in his body. "Thanks, Jack."

Disconnecting he turned to find Gunner standing behind him. The look on his face was unreadable. "We have a traitor?" he asked with what looked like barely controlled anger.

Alex looked around to see if anyone was close before he answered. "Yes, it looks that way."

"Do we know who it is?"

Alex shook his head in frustration. "No, and this stays strictly between us. I can't have all the men looking over their shoulders. It's bad enough I am."

"Fuck." And there was that word again.

"Yeah, fuck," he said tiredly.

"Let me know what I can do to help. This shit doesn't fly." Gunner didn't look happy as he adjusted his sling.

"Yeah, will do. For now, I just want Evelyn back."

"Yeah, I get that. I like her, she's good for you. You're a lucky man," Gunner said with a chuckle.

"Yeah, I am." But he didn't fucking deserve her. He should have kept her safe and he hadn't. The phone rang in his hand and he lifted it. "I need to take this," he stated making it clear he wanted privacy and Gunner nodded before moving back inside while Alex watched. "Alex."

"You have Lucy, Jace, Roz, K, and Daniel on their way. They should be there by lunchtime."

Relief washed through Alex at the first good sign he'd had since he let Evelyn leave his side. "Thank you, Jack." After a short conversation confirming the details, he ended the call. When he got Evelyn back, he was tying her to the bed and leaving her there where she would be safe.

CHAPTER TWENTY-SEVEN

RAIN WAS BEGINNING TO FALL AS THE MORNING MOVED INTO early afternoon. The clouds were heavy in the sky as Alex watched the drops hit the glass of the patio doors. They had planned all they could until the others from Fortis arrived, so he told everyone to get a few hours sleep. He wasn't taking his own advice of course; he couldn't rest knowing the woman he loved, the person who his entire world turned for, was in the clutches of a man known for death and the cruellest of torture.

He lifted the coffee to his lips and took a sip grimacing at the cold sludge before moving away from the window towards the kitchen. He passed the front door of the beautiful home and paused as he heard a vehicle pull up. Placing the mug down on a glass entrance table he took his gun from the waistband of his trousers and held it at his side as he approached the door and the window to the side.

Relief flooded him and for the first time since this began, he felt a little lighter. Lucy, Jace, Roz, and Kanan alighted from a seven-seater MPV, followed by Daniel from the front. The first four were couples, and both women were linked to Zenobi.

Roz was the leader of that fucking scary group of female assassins while Lucy had left Zenobi and now worked for Fortis with her brother Dane. The likeness between the siblings was unmistakable, as was the affection. Jace, Lucy's fiancé, was ex-SAS and had worked with Dane which was how he and Lucy met. K and Roz had a much more complicated story, but he hadn't heard the whole thing and wasn't sure exactly what their history was. What wasn't in any doubt was how much Kanan adored his abrasive wife.

He was the only man he knew brave enough to sleep next to the woman without fear of his balls being cut off. Dane and Daniel were best friends and both ex-SAS. Daniel had recently got engaged to Dane's baby sister Megan, and they were expecting their first child together. He was also the team's medic and Alex prayed to God he wouldn't need him but knew that prayer was probably going to go unanswered.

Alex pulled open the door and smiled at the group who were walking towards him before stepping back inside to let them enter. He tucked his weapon away and held out a hand to Daniel. "Thanks for coming, Daniel."

Daniel took his hand and shook it firmly. Daniel was tall, as were all the men in the Fortis group. At just shy of forty he was also in prime physical shape with the added benefit of experience on his side. With dark hair and brown eyes, he'd had his share of women but was now happily settled with the love of his life. They'd had a difficult time getting there but it was clear to see that his life was now pretty fucking perfect.

"Don't mention it, anything we can do to help." Daniel dumped his bag on the floor and looked around.

"Alex." Lucy stepped forward and hugged him tight before pulling back and looking at him as she held his biceps so she could assess him.

"Thanks for coming, Luce."

"We'll get her back, Alex. Evelyn is strong and clever. She'll keep herself as safe as can be until we get to her."

"Thanks, Luce." Alex turned then to shake Jace's hand before saying hello to Kanan and Daniel.

Both men were quiet, but Daniel, the darker of the two was the thinker, the more level headed leader. Kanan was also ex-SIS and still had his ear to the ground. He felt Roz beside him and turned to the leader of Zenobi and the woman who had lied to Evelyn. Roz was tall, slender, toned, and stunning in a biker chick I-will-eat-your-heart-for-breakfast-if-you-fuck-with-me kind of way. Her almost black hair was short and shaved into her neck but longer on top. She had almond-shaped eyes and a tongue that could cut you as fast as the deadly knives she carried.

"Alex."

"Roz."

"I fucked up. I admit it, but I'll fix it and anyone who tries to stop me will have their intestines dragged out through their teeth," she vowed.

He could see the truth and the guilt in her face. It was as close as he would ever get to an apology, but he didn't need one. He needed Evelyn back.

"Kitten." Kanan slipped an arm around Roz's belly and pulled her back to his chest as he bent his head to her neck. "Play nice."

"I was fucking playing nice," she hissed but with less heat.

Alex watched her face soften slightly as she listened to whatever Kanan was whispering into her neck.

"She's just upset," Kanan defended.

"Understood. Shall we get you settled and then I can bring you up to speed?"

"Sure."

Alex could sense Daniel was watching him closely. He guessed Daniel was wondering how close to the edge he was. Alex sighed internally, not sure himself, and showed them into the now more crowded than ever office space.

"Show me where the kitchen is and I'll grab some coffee for us all," Lucy said. "Roz come help me."

"Do I look like a fucking slave?" Roz raised a perfectly arched eyebrow.

"I would do anything for a caffeine hit."

Roz spun and pinned Kanan with a look. "Anything? Even attend that fucking god-awful Easter play the girls are in at school with me?"

Alex tried not to laugh despite the situation.

"Even that, my love."

"Come on, Luce. Let's get the man a coffee." She shooed Lucy out of the room.

"I already got the tickets for the play but don't tell her."

A few minutes later Roz and Lucy returned with coffee and biscuits on a tray looking like the most badass servers in the world wearing leather jackets, skin-tight jeans, and shit-kickers on their feet. It was surreal but it pulled Alex out of his fog enough to feel energised.

Blake, Reid, and Liam joined them, shortly after that Gunner and Pax appeared.

"Ma'am." Reid gave a slow nod as he passed Roz.

"Don't you fucking *Ma'am* me. I ain't your fucking mother."

Reid smirked as did Liam.

Kanan rolled his eyes and stroked a finger down her face before handing her a cup. "Drink your coffee, Kitten."

Alex shook his head wondering again how the man did it. "Now everyone is here we need to finish this plan and then get on the road. It is six hours to Livorno and the last ferry to Capraia is seven tonight. So, the window is incredibly short."

"What's the plan?"

Alex looked at Daniel. "We go in on the ferry as a tourist

group. There's one restaurant and a small family run hotel. I've booked us all reservations using aliases under the guise that we're there for a fortieth birthday celebration. We're going to go in under different couple combo's so as not to alert anyone to a large group of single men entering the island. Blake will partner Pax again, Roz and K, Lucy and Jace. You and the rest of us will go in as singles.

"Once there we'll split up. The house is located towards the back of the island and has a large perimeter fence. We need to breach it and go in quiet. I don't want this fucker spooked and try to use Evelyn as a shield. I'll take the lead." Alex looked around the room. "Daniel and Reid, I want you to focus on finding Evelyn and getting her the fuck out of there. Liam and Blake, I want Osiris. I don't fucking want that bastard to get away. The rest of you are on clean-up. I want all the guards taken out and I don't care how. Everyone clear?"

"What about me?" The question came from Gunner.

"I want you as the watchman. I need to know if we're going to get company." He knew it was the shit job, but with Gunner wounded, he didn't have much choice.

"Really?" Gunner asked on a groan.

"Sorry, man. You're injured and I can't have you in there. You'd be a liability."

"It's only a fucking shoulder shot."

"Can you move your arm with full range?" Daniel scrutinised the sling Gunner wore.

"No, but..."

"No buts. You're on watch." Alex made sure his voice was firm stopping any further arguments. "Right, let's get on the road."

The drive to Livorno was reasonably uneventful. Pax had decided to go with Roz and Lucy which left Blake, a sulky Gunner, Reid, and Liam in their car. With five men it was a bit of a tight squeeze, but the Land Rover Discovery was a rental and a good cover. Plus, it had plenty of room in the back for their weapons.

Alex dozed off for an hour. With Liam driving his body was finally able to shut down for a bit now there was no more planning to be done. He was startled awake with images of a bloody Evelyn screaming through his brain from a nightmare. Her hands had been reaching for him and he wasn't able to get to her. His heart was hammering in his chest as he gulped in a couple of breaths of air to calm his wild pulse.

"You good?" Blake asked from beside him.

"Yeah. Fine." He looked out the window and noticed they were an hour out from Livorno and making much better time than expected.

"I'm sorry about before. I would never choose a woman over the team. I hope you know that."

"You haven't met the right woman then because I would choose Evelyn over everything," Alex said honestly.

"I can't imagine having that."

Alex thought he heard regret in his voice. "No, you can't but when you find it, you won't be able to imagine life without it."

Blake said nothing in response just nodded and turned to hassle Reid who was reading a book about meditation.

Alex half listened as the two bull-shitted with each other, his hands itching to get there and get started. He thought about all the nights he had spent with Evelyn—making love to her, holding her while they filled in the blanks from the last fifteen years, her giggle when he found a ticklish spot and how that had turned into making love until they were both exhausted.

Watching her paint, her head tilting from one side to the next as she tried to find the perfect angle or colour. Her stealing a slice of bacon straight out of the pan and dipping it in syrup while he laughed at her impatience. The images were seared into his brain, tiny moments of beauty that he wanted more of. He wanted to spend a lifetime making small moments. Watching her get round with their child, teaching him or her to paint or fight, or God forbid, cook.

He needed that future with her more than he needed to breathe. The pain was so intense that he had to block it and bury it deep where it couldn't cloud his thinking. He wouldn't pretend she was just another mission because he couldn't. She was fucking everything and if he had to kill every person on that island to save her that was precisely what he would do.

———

HER THROAT WAS like a sand dune in the desert sun. Her mouth felt swollen as she tried to swallow with very little saliva. Her body hurt to the point her mind was shutting it out, shutting down her pain receptors. Osiris had returned an hour after the first beating and seemed angry—colder somehow than before he'd left.

He had nodded at Irish who had moved forward and with an almost apologetic look slammed his fist into her face. The pain exploded in her cheek as white dots danced in her vision. It hurt like a bitch, but she sensed he was holding back. The next one was to her ribs and belly making her cough as she struggled to catch her breath.

"Are you going to cooperate, Evelyn?" Osiris asked calmly.

"Fuck you," she hissed and spat the blood from her mouth at his feet.

"Very well."

She could sense the anger vibrating off him because she wouldn't do as she was told. He turned and stepped towards the door as a second man walked in. This one was smaller, almost skinny and shorter than the others. But he scared her more than Irish did. Irish had life in his eyes, this man did not. He moved towards her, the suit he wore almost hanging off him like a young boy playing dress up and he wasn't far short of that age group either.

"This is Nick. He is very fond of blades and he's going to help me persuade you to be more respectful." Osiris stepped back as did Irish after a brief hesitation.

Evelyn sucked in her breath and tried not to let her racing heart send her into a tailspin of panic.

The blade was long and thin—a wickedly sharp looking butcher's filleting knife if she wasn't mistaken. She kept her eyes on it as it moved towards her neck going deadly still, knowing the slightest wrong move and her jugular would be opened and cover the walls in her blood. The knife moved towards the neckline of her shirt as she kept her eyes on Nick, his soulless black eyes glinting like a snake.

She felt the fabric part as it was cut like a hot knife through butter until she was exposed from her chest to her bellybutton. The first cut made her wince as the sharp blade opened her skin just under the curve of her right breast. The trickle of blood felt warm on her chilled skin as it slid down her tummy into the waistband of her leggings. The next was a centimetre down and as it continued Evelyn fought to block out the stinging pain.

Determined not to show them any tears her mind instead went to Alex—Alex who would be fucking furious when he saw her skin was cut and her face and ribs were bloodied and bruised. Alex who cooked honey panna cotta for her just because he knew it was her favourite or left little notes around the flat for her to find. The man who would sit for hours and watch her paint. The man who made love to her like she was the most precious woman in the world and then fucked her hard and rough because he seemed to know what she needed before even she did. Who allowed her to be soft and feminine while still seeing her as strong and independent, never making her be anything other than who she was.

The man she loved more than anything, the man who had

owned her heart since she was six. She knew he would find her, she knew he would kill them for touching her, so she endured and blocked the pain not allowing them to see her hurt or her fear.

She watched dimly as Nick walked away, finished for the moment with carving her body up. Osiris followed him out, disgust written on his face. Irish paused for a second before moving back to her. She watched him through one eye as the other began to close with swelling. He reached for her chest and she couldn't fight the flinch. She could take the pain but the thought of another man putting his hand on her was too much.

He didn't touch her though, rather he pulled the two sides of the shirt together, covering her as he tied them in a knot.

"Why are you doing this?" She couldn't understand why Irish was acting so strange.

"It's my job," he said and walked away but as she waited, she didn't hear the clank of the lock slide shut. Not that she was able to do anything about it. Weak from the beatings and now blood loss, she could hardly unhook herself and get free, especially suffering from dehydration as she was.

Evelyn stayed like that for what seemed like hours, her mind wandering back over her life and what she wanted out of it in the future. She was tired of being Siren. Seducing men to get them to spill their secrets was not the job for a woman in her thirties. She wanted a family and to paint and burn meals for her incredibly handsome and sexy husband who would sweep her off her feet and tell her she was the most beautiful creature alive even with bed hair and morning breath. She grew hot and sweat began to drip down her face and neck over the next few hours and she thought that perhaps she had gotten an infection from one of the cuts. Her head felt heavy on her neck as she fought to stay conscious.

Loud noises were coming from above her and she wondered if perhaps it was the fourth of July. She'd always loved fireworks as a girl. Her father would always let her have some at her birthday party. God, she missed her father. She had always been a daddy's girl and it had been so long since she had been held by him.

The noise got closer and she heard shouting and screaming followed by boots running. Suddenly the door slammed open and Alex was there. His hands on her, his voice as he whispered to her, reassuring and gentle as he lifted her down and into his arms. She turned and the pain was immense, but it didn't matter to her because he was here, and she was safe now. Evelyn let everything else go, the pain, the fear, all of it as she allowed blissful uncon-sciousness to overtake her. Alex had her now and that was all that mattered.

CHAPTER TWENTY-EIGHT

THE WARMTH OF FAMILIAR ARMS AROUND HER, THE SCENT OF him surrounding her as he held her was the first thing Evelyn noticed as she came around. Safe. She was safe! Evelyn took a moment to enjoy that feeling, relishing in it even. Taking a tentative breath, she realised that her ribs didn't hurt as much as she thought they would. Despite her delirium at the end of her kidnapping she remembered everything that had been done to her. She probably would for years to come.

Her hand snaked up over her belly touching the gauze that covered the cuts on her ribcage. Little reminders of a man she'd thought was her friend, a man she had loved but had turned out to be nothing but a criminal and a sick man that tried to justify what he had done. Good men that did terrible things, she understood that. But Arthur—or David—as she thought of him, was evil.

Raising her head slightly she glanced around her surroundings. The room she was in was like a hotel suite. She was in a double bed and a thick quilt covered her instead of sheets. There were flowers on a nightstand, and a small sofa and table with magazines on them, but it was clean and sterile. Probably a private hospital she guessed.

She was laying on her back with Alex on his side facing her, his one hand placed gently over her tummy, the tips of his fingers curving around her hip, his other arm was under her neck, her head resting on his bicep, as if he was scared to let her out of his arms. As she turned her head, she saw his long lashes lying against his cheeks as he slept. Dark shadows underneath were evidence of the fear and sleeplessness he had suffered in her absence.

Lifting her arm, she ran her hand over the scruff on his cheek, the stubble catching on the pads of her fingers. His hair was standing up as if he had run his hands through it time and again. His eyes fluttered open and she smiled and then winced slightly at the pain in her cheek.

"Hey," she said softly as he looked at her with so much love in his eyes.

"Hey, you." His smile made tears prick her eyes. She had wondered when Osiris had her if she would ever see that smile again. Alex sat up at the sight of her tears. "What's this?" He swept the tears away with his thumbs before gently cupping her face.

"I thought I would never see you again." She wept as he took her in his arms and held her tightly with her head on his chest, his strong arms around her body.

"I will always come for you, *mi nena*," he vowed while she cried in his arms until there were no tears left to cry and finally her emotions were under control.

"What happened?" She lifted her head and met his eyes.

"You have bruised ribs and a broken cheekbone. The cuts on your torso were infected so they gave you a huge dose of antibiotics when you came in and put you on IV fluids for dehydration. It will all heal but it will take time and rest. Can you remember what happened?" She could sense the abject fear in his voice when he asked the question.

"Yes, one of the guards—an Irishman I think—beat me, but I think he was holding back for some reason."

"If what he did to you is holding back, he better hope I never find him," Alex said savagely as he caressed her face.

"I bet I look a sight." She lifted a hand to her face, lightly touching what she knew were bruises.

"Most beautiful woman in the world." Alex grinned and she knew he meant every word, but she still laughed lightly causing a twinge in her ribs.

"Who cut you?"

"A man named Nick. He was scrawny and seemed young, but he was dead inside. Alex, I have never seen such dead eyes."

"Did anyone..." Alex stumbled over his words.

"No." She rushed to reassure him, knowing what he feared and wanting to reassure him straight away.

"Thank God," he said on a loud exhale.

"Did they get away?"

Osiris and the Irishman you describe did. Nick, and I'm assuming it was Nick, was killed along with the rest of his men on the island.

"Were any of our guys hurt? I saw Gunner fall into the sea..." She let her words trail off. The gentle giant who looked like a Viking had been so sweet to her and she didn't want to think he was hurt, or worse.

"Gunner took a round to the shoulder, but he's fine if a little bit of a grump. Reid took a knife slash to the gut, but he's more pissed about it ruining his ink than hurt."

"So, what happens now?"

"Well, I gave the data that Booth stole back to the head of security at the Palace who flew in specially. The hit has been officially called off and you're no longer a suspect."

"Do we know how Simon knew about Princess Caitlin not being Royal?"

"We understand he was sleeping with one of the maids at Kensington and she told him there had been rumours. We assume the rest he found out on his own. He had access to the Palace and the people so it's not much of a jump."

"And Booth now?" she asked knowing there was more to this story but already feeling exhaustion pulling at her.

"He's dead."

"Really? How?"

"I killed him." He seemed to pause as he waited for her reaction. "He would never have given up and I won't have you living under a cloud of fear, constantly watching your back."

"You killed him for me." She stroked a finger over his chest as he kissed her head.

"I would tear down the world for you, Evelyn."

"Who said romance was dead." The familiar voice from the door made her look up with a grin.

"Lucy!" Evelyn exclaimed with a happy smile.

Lucy walked in with Jace behind her. She and Lucy were similar in looks and had worked many jobs together before Luce went to work for Fortis.

"What are you doing here?" she asked as Lucy moved to hug and kiss her as she sat up slowly.

"Heard you had some trouble and your man here needed back up. Couldn't let these guys have all the fun."

Jace moved in and kissed her cheek. "Good to see you, Evelyn. Sorry about the circumstances though."

"So, you flew out to help rescue me?" she said feeling the love from everyone around her.

Lucy smiled. "Not just us. Daniel, Roz, and Kanan did too."

"Roz is here?"

"She is but she doesn't want to see you. She has some major guilt going on."

Evelyn felt Alex's arms tighten around her at Lucy's words before he sighed. "I haven't got to that bit yet."

Lucy formed a perfect O with her mouth and then rolled her lips into her teeth looking awkward.

"How about we go, and you can do that." Jace took Lucy's hand and pulled her towards the door.

"I'll see you soon. You'll come to the wedding, right?" Lucy asked them both.

"Hell, yes. Try and stop us."

Her friend was radiant, so in love with her fiancé, the man she had pined over for years before he got his act together.

She waited a beat after the door closed before she spoke. "Roz knew, didn't she? About David being Osiris?"

"Yes, she did."

"Is that why you and Pax fell out before we left?"

"Yeah, she just hit me with it, and I had to lie to you. I hated it but I didn't want to compromise the mission as it was our only way to clear your name and get the target off your back."

She could hear the guilt and the anger in his voice. "It's okay, Alex. I would have done the same, and she put you in an awkward position which we will have to talk about, but I don't blame you. All you've done since this began is protect me and I love you for it." Emotion in every word

"I love you too, Evelyn." There was a comfortable silence as they both realised that for the first time since they had been reunited, they were free to move on with their lives.

"So, what now?" she asked feeling like a scared child.

"Now we live our life together wherever you want that to be. I finally put a wedding ring on your finger, a baby in your belly, and we grow old loving each other."

"Was that a proposal?" Her heart started to beat faster.

"No, baby. I did that fifteen years ago and I'm holding you to it." He held the ring he'd found in her bag, the same one he had given her so long ago. He slipped it on her finger and kissed her softly.

Evelyn felt her body quicken as desire flooded her. She grinned at him. "How soon can we get out of here and start that?"

"Whenever you want, baby. Whenever you want."

Evelyn melted as he dotted sweet drugging kisses down her neck and almost forgot about her wounds, wincing when she tried to take things too far too fast.

"Time to sleep, *mi nena*." Alex pulled away and dropped a sweet kiss on her nose.

She grumbled but felt sleep pulling her under as her mind tried to keep up. "When I'm healed, I want to go home, Alex."

"To Paris?"

"To Miami. I want to see my parents again. It's time."

"Okay, baby, we can do that." He gave her a squeeze. "Now sleep."

"Okay." She was quiet for a few minutes. "Alex?"

"Yes, baby?" Evelyn could hear the humour in his voice.

"What are we going to do about Osiris and the traitor at Eidolon?" The threat was still on her mind even as she lay safe in his arms.

"Don't you worry about either of them. I have a feeling neither will be a problem for long."

"Do you know who it is?"

"Not yet but I'm getting closer and have it narrowed down. Now sleep, baby. I won't go anywhere."

"Love you."

"Love you too, *mi nena*," he whispered as she drifted off.

EPILOGUE

Evelyn's hand felt like it was trying to crush his as they pulled up outside the small, two-bedroom, single story home with the whitewashed façade and bright yellow shutters. It had been a month since Evelyn's kidnapping, and she was almost completely healed. She had the occasional nightmare but other than that she was fine. They talked about it very little now. Evelyn seemed determined to put that part of her life behind her.

Alex was not fairing so well. He still woke up in sweats of fear, his hands finding her in the dark as he tried to convince himself she was safe. She was as safe as he could make her, but Osiris was still a threat.

He had met with Roz a week after the attack and Roz had told him that the mistake was hers and she would be the one to find him and personally take him down. One of her girls getting hurt was not something she handled well. Despite his anger at her he knew she had done what she had with the best intentions.

He had received a text that morning from her with two words.

`Target Eliminated.`

It had brought with it an immense amount of relief and he would tell Evelyn later that night when they were alone but right now, they were sitting in the car outside her childhood home. Evelyn looked beautiful in a vibrant yellow dress with orange and blue flowers that fell to her knees. The cap sleeves and sweetheart neckline showed off her curves but still made her look like the young girl he had fallen in love with.

"Ready, *mi nena?*" He brought their clasped hands to his lips and kissed her hand.

Her eyes that had been glued to the house turned to him and they glistened with emotion. "I'm scared. What if they don't want to know me?"

"They want to know you, Evelyn. They never stopped missing you. *Look!*"

He pointed to the door as it slowly opened to reveal her mama and papa. They were older and greyer, but they looked the same. Evelyn's hand flew to her mouth as a noise escaped her. Alex nudged her and then exited the car and came around to help her out as she seemed to have forgotten how to move.

"Mama, Papa," she whispered her voice full of unshed tears.

"*My baby.*"

He could see her mother mouthing the words and then Evelyn was running, and she was in her mother's arms, her father holding the two women he loved as they wept and talked over each other. He stood back and watched the reunion, not wanting to intrude knowing what this meant to them all.

"Alex," Evelyn called and ushered him over as she swiped at the tears on her cheeks.

"Alejandro, come." Her father shook Alex's hand clasping it in both of his and shaking. "Thank you for bringing our girl back to us." He was watching as his daughter and wife walked into their home with a massive smile on his face. They followed behind and both men stopped in the living room to give the two women a moment alone as mother and daughter made their way to the kitchen.

"It wasn't me. Evelyn fought her way back to us. Your daughter is strong and fierce." He smiled as they entered the small colourful home, the walls a bright terracotta the tile to match.

"Like her mama."

"Yes." She was. They looked alike and both a had a formidable spirit which he thanked God for.

"You will wed now?" Evelyn's father asked as he looked at Alex before nodding. "You will wed now." He hadn't waited for Alex to reply but grinned as he clapped him on the back. Apparently reading Alex's expression was all he needed.

"Do I have your blessing?" Alex wanted to be sure and respected these people enough to want their blessing.

"You had my blessing fifteen years ago, Alejandro."

Alex felt his eyes go wide before he chuckled. You never could get one over on a Cuban parent. They stayed for the rest of the afternoon as they caught up, his mother joining them which prompted more tears from the women. It was the perfect day, although he couldn't wait to get her alone that night and have her all to himself.

———

HEREFORD, THE UNITED KINGDOM

HE SLIPPED AWAY from the people at the bar and headed around the corner to make the call. The text had come in five minutes ago and he knew not to keep them waiting. Bile and self-loathing crept through him as he thought of what he had done and what he still had to do before he could find a way out of the mess he found himself in.

The burner phone rang as he waited in the rain.

"You took too long," was the greeting.

"I couldn't get away." He hated defending himself but knew if he didn't, people he cared about would die.

"Do you have what I need?"

"No. I need more time." The door behind him swung open and a group of rowdy lads fell out of the bar half pissed and laughing and he jumped. He felt his heart kick up knowing that it was only a matter of time before he got caught.

"You have one week to give me something useful or you won't like the consequences. I have already proven to you that I can get to you and your team by nearly putting that Garcia bitch in the ground. It was easy to set her up and it would be easy to set up another innocent to draw them out."

"I know. I tried. I gave you the information on Michaela Kirk and that operation. How was I to know she would fuck it up?" He had known she would of course, because he was in part responsible for stopping her, he had helped to secure her in France.

"Not good enough. I want the details on the next mission in my inbox by Friday or the next thing you do will be picking up the body parts of your team members."

The phone went dead in his hand and he looked at it wanting to smash it and knowing he couldn't. The threat was clear. Either he provided information on Eidolon Ops or the team would be killed but not before their families had been tortured. He had thought it was bullshit. Nobody could get near Eidolon but by setting Evelyn up and pitting Simon Booth against Osiris they had proved they had the power and means.

Now he needed to get himself out of this hole before his team caught him or someone died. First though, he needed to figure out who was blackmailing him and what their endgame was.

Running his hand through his hair he sighed and schooled his features before walking back inside the pub.

"Hey, come on slow coach. It's your round." Jack shouted.

"Yeah coming." He laughed at his teammate as he took out his wallet and went to the bar.

———

TWO YEARS LATER

"Do you think they'll like it? *Oh, God.* They're going to hate them. I can't do it, Alex. I think I'm going to puke."

"Just calm down, *mi nena.* Everyone is going to love them, how could they not?"

He looked around *The Athena Art Gallery* and the paintings hanging on the walls. Each one painted by the new up and coming artist Evelyn Martinez. The gallery that was owned by Zenobi had become real instead of a front. One in France and one in Hereford both were fronts for Zenobi offices still but having seen Evelyn's artwork and using Pax's contacts Roz had decided to actually allow some exhibitions. This was the night that would launch Evelyn's career as an artist, and he couldn't be prouder of her. Hunter and Lexi McKenzie had flown in from their home in the USA, Delphine and Thomas had come in a few days ago from Paris, Will and Aubrey—as well as most of the guys from Eidolon and their partners—and everyone from Zenobi had come to share Evelyn's success.

Roz and Evelyn had taken a while to iron out their differences but now were stronger than ever. Roz had apologised for lying to Evelyn about David being Osiris and explained that it was only Pax she had told. Her reasons for doing what she had done were still unclear, but his opinion was that Roz had control issues, but he and Evelyn didn't discuss it any more as it only caused arguments that he would not let affect his life.

"Do you think so?"

He cupped her shoulders in his palms to steady her. "Look at me, Evelyn," he demanded." The demand was clear, and her eyes flew to his and he saw the instant desire in them at his firm tone. "Everyone is going to love your paintings. The tickets have been sold out for months."

"I know. It's just...This means a lot to me."

"I know it does, *mi nena*," he said." He softened his voice seeing the self-doubt in her eyes. He took her hand and led her towards the painting that was the star of the show. The gallery was empty except for them. The food had been provided by Delphine and Thomas, the gallery manager had left to change, and as Alex was in charge of security it left just the two of them.

He held her in front of him, her back to his front as they stood in front of the painting he loved the most. It epitomised the two of them—the before, the after, and the still to come.

"Do you remember the night you started this painting?" He ran his hands down the sides of her body before moving up to cup her full breasts. He felt her relax into him on a sigh of desire, her breath quickening.

"Of course, it was the night this one was conceived." She rubbed her hand over her very pregnant belly. Alex caressed her belly as well, the love for this woman who was his wife and the child that would soon enter their lives almost overwhelming in its intensity.

He kissed his way down her neck as she angled it to give him better access. "Yes, and do you remember what you said when it was finished?"

"That it was the story of us. Our love story."

"How then can that not be the most beautiful thing you have ever seen?" He turned her in his arms so she was plastered against him. The sexy curve of her breasts were trying to break free of the Grecian style midnight blue dress that flowed to her ankles and the flat sandals he had insisted she wear. They'd had words about that, but he had won that particular battle. His life was full of love and beauty and even the arguments were perfect because he got to have make up sex with the siren he called 'wife'.

Alex's head came down and he took her mouth in a hot wet kiss that had her moaning into his mouth as her body pressed closer wanting more. His cock hardened beneath the tux he wore as she wiggled against him. He pulled back and saw the passion and need in her eyes.

"Ever fucked in an Art Gallery?" He smirked as he took her hand and pulled her towards the back of the gallery where they could have some privacy.

"Alex!" She giggled but he knew she was as eager as he was.

Yes, his life was perfect, and he would not change anything about the heartache that had plagued him for fifteen years because it led him to his perfect life.

SNEAK PEEK: BLAKE

AN EIDOLON BLACK OPS NOVEL: BOOK 2

Three Years Ago

BLAKE SLAMMED HIS hand down on the desk anger making his fist shake as he tried to control it. He glared at the woman across from him who had given the order that had nearly go his principal killed. "This was a fucking shit show, and you know it. I should never have been moved at such late notice and swapped out for some fucking green kid."

Blake paced, his hands threading through his short blonde hair in frustrating at the situation. The woman opposite looked at him calmly, barely a hair out of place, her suit wrinkle free as if she was ready for church. Nothing like a woman who had nearly gotten the Queen murdered with her incompetence.

"I understand you're upset."

Blake spun on his heel to face her. "Upset? Are you fucking with me right now? I'm fucking livid. Whose idea was it to swap me out for that FNG?"

"I am not aware what FNG means," replied Commander Helen Pope with a dangerous edge to her tone that made Blake stop.

Blake leaned into the desk making the woman stand and face him not backing down an inch. "It means fucking new guy!"

"Yes, well, to answer your question it was not my idea. The order came directly from the Deputy Commissioner." She sighed and sat back in her chair. "Listen, Blake, you're a good officer, the best we have. So no, I don't know what's going on, but I intend to find out." She looked at him sternly then. "But if you raise your voice to me again, I'll have you demoted back down to Police Constable before you can even blink."

Her tone made Blake sit back down opposite her, his anger at her leaving him and his next words were sincere, "Fine. I apologise."

He had a lot of respect for Helen Pope. She had worked her way up the ladder in a very male dominated job. Not only had she done well for herself, but she had done a lot of good within the police force and especially with Protection Command.

"Is she okay?" he asked knowing that she may not tell him.

Blake took his job as PPO very seriously. These people relied on him to keep them safe while they went about their jobs and lives. The only way to do that was to build a rapport with them, gain some trust, and he had done that. Now the new Deputy Commissioner had come in and decided that the PPOs would work on a rota system. Each officer would take turns protecting different people.

"Yes. She is resting comfortably in her suite at Balmoral. It wasn't your fault, Blake. This rests with me."

"No, it doesn't and you and I both know it. This new system is dangerous and it's going to get someone killed." He took in a breath. "I'm not sure I can watch that happen." He leaned back on his heels, his hands crossed in front of him as he delivered those words.

"What are you saying, Blake?" Commander Pope asked directly.

"That I'm tendering my resignation with immediate effect."

He watched as a flicker of emotion flew across the Commander's face. She was an attractive woman, and at fifty was still in prime fitness. She had even been known to take one of her men down to the mat in practice. She wore her greyish blonde hair pinned back in a tight bun at the back of her neck and never gave in to female fripperies like make-up. She was a hardass, but he respected her and enjoyed working for her, but he couldn't work under the new commissioner and the new guidelines which all but guaranteed he would be attending a state funeral at some point.

"That seems rather hasty," she said slowly her hands resting on the desk, her fingers peaked.

"It might be, but I've given it careful consideration. I can't in good conscience do this job if I feel I'm compromising the safety of those around me, most especially the principal. I either do this properly or not at all."

Pope nodded. "I see. We will be very sorry to lose you, Blake. It goes without saying that your commitment and drive on the force will be sorely missed. That said, I do understand and if you ever change your mind, you know where I am."

"Thank you, Commander, it has been an honour to serve under you," he said with genuine feeling.

"I will have your papers drawn up, but I need your shield and firearm."

Blake produced both and with only the slightest feeling of reverence placed them down on her desk. He raised his hand as she stood and saluted her which she returned. "Ma'am," He dropped his hand turned to leave.

"Blake."

He turned back to her. "Yes, Ma'am?"

"Do you know what you will do now?"

He shook his head. "Not a clue," he said with a grin that had turned many a woman to mush.

She nodded but was unaffected by his charm. She went to her desk and jotted down a number on a piece of paper and handed it to him. "Give this guy a call. He's putting together a team, and I have a feeling you would be a good fit. He's a bit of a stubborn hardass but a good man with good morals. Tell him I sent you."

"Thank you, Ma'am," Blake replied and looked down at the card in his hand.

In her elegant, feminine handwriting she had written *Jack Granger* 07892 778 923.

Blake left the Scotland Yard building for the final time and shoved the card in the back pocket of his black trousers. He would give him a call, maybe. But first, he wanted to check for himself that the Monarch, Queen Lydia II was in fact okay.

Taking his phone from his pocket, he dialled the number he knew by heart and waited.

"Hello?"

"It's me. Is she okay?" he asked not beating around the bush.

"Yes, she will be. She's a bit shaken, but the Duke is on his way home and should be here in due course."

"Good. Listen, tell her to take care and if you need anything just ask."

"I will tell her," the man on the other end of the phone said.

Blake hung up and sighed. He felt like he was abandoning a good woman and her family, leaving them to fend for themselves, but he couldn't be part of cost-cutting that put people in danger. Pulling at the tie around his neck he headed to the tube. He needed a week off, a willing woman, and a large bottle of Vodka. Then he would see what his future held.

BOOKS BY MADDIE WADE

Fortis Security

Healing Danger

Stolen Dreams

Love Divided

Secret Redemption

Broken Butterfly

Arctic Fire

Phoenix Rising

Nate & Skye Wedding Novella

Digital Desire

Eidolon Black Ops

Alex

Blake (Coming Soon)

Alliance Agency Series (co-written with India Kells)

Deadly Alliance

Knight Watch (Coming soon)

Tightrope Duet

Tightrope One

Tightrope Two

CONTACT ME

If stalking an author is your thing and I sure hope it is, then here are the links to my social media pages.

If you prefer your stalking to be more intimate then my group Maddie's Minxes will welcome you with open arms.

General Email: info.maddiewade@gmail.com

Email: maddie@maddiewadeauthor.co.uk

Website: http://www.maddiewadeauthor.co.uk

Facebook page: https://www.facebook.com/maddieuk/

Facebook group: https://www.facebook.com/groups/546325035557882/

Amazon Author page: amazon.com/author/maddiewade

Goodreads: https://www.goodreads.com/author/show/14854265.Maddie_Wade

Bookbub: https://partners.bookbub.com/authors/3711690/edit

Twitter:@mwadeauthor

Pinterest:@maddie_wade

Instagram:Maddie Author